Unmasked:
Erotic Tales
of
Gay Superheroes

An Anthology Edited By
Eric Summers

STARbooks
PRESS
Herndon, VA

Herndon, VA

Unmasked: Erotic Tales of Gay Superheroes

An Anthology Edited By
Eric Summers

STARbooks PRESS
Herndon, VA

Contents

Acknowledgements

Thank you to all the wonderful contributors to *Unmasked: Erotic Tales of Gay Superheroes*. The response to our submission call was so overwhelming that we regret we were unable to include everyone. Working with this talented group of writers was a pleasure, and I look forward to working with them on future anthologies.

– Eric Summers

Eric Summers Anthologies from STARbooks Press

Muscle Worshipers
Love in a Lock-Up

Tights
By DesertMac

"I'm gonna lose it if I don't get a decent costume made soon! I'm so fuckin' tired of my tights ripping or sagging off after only one or two uses ... not to mention the threat of a lawsuit for indecent exposure!"

"Seriously, Span buddy, like I was telling ya, this kid's the best; WaspMan recommended him to me. With this guy's suits, mine only get torn up in fights with really high-powered suvils."

SpanMan sipped his Supo Big Gulp and sighed at OwlMan. "OK, OK, I'll give him a try." He shook his head, looking around the half empty SUPOdiner in League City, dinnertime home of so many of the supos of The League of Super Heroes.

"I guarantee you'll like him, especially if you've been to supotailors like this guy I went to once." he shuddered. "The fruit was groping me here, feeling me there ... I almost tore into his neck with my omnibeak. I just don't like a guy touching me all over, y'know?" OwlMan frowned and furrowed his feathered brow. "But, this kid is OK. Not a grope or a lisp anywhere in sight. He's alright."

SpanMan eyed him warily. "Ummm, yeah, I know what ya mean. The gays really get into us supos, but hey, can ya blame 'em?" He grinned, and the light shimmered off what was left of his metallic-spandex tights as he flexed his muscles.

"Oh, yeah," OwlMan smirked, "And the gay supos? Don't get me started!"

OwlMan fluffed his feathers and started to say something, but SpanMan covered his ears and begged, "No! No! Don't start! Please!" OwlMan flattened his feathers back down.

"Sorry," he said.

They both stood, carried their food trays to the trash bin and dumped the refuse. SpanMan looked away and held his breath so as not to have to smell the remains of OwlMan's aged mouse morsels. He held out his GPS Blueberry and said, "Well, punch his coords in for me, and I'll check him out."

OwlMan punched in the coordinates and said, "He lives up in the mountains above Perilopolis, out in the middle of nowhere. Not an endangered owl habitat in sight."

"OK, I'll go up this morning. I have to drop by the SUPOsitory and draw out some money, then I'll glide on up there. I've got to snag me a good tailor now. As it is, the skin showing in my last pair of tights here already gets comments of, 'Look! Up in the sky! It's SkinMan!'" He shook his head and sighed as he and OwlMan went their separate ways.

* * * * *

Wes looked in the mirror and flexed his slender body as he dried off after his shower. He thought, "Damn lot of workouts going to waste here. Dunno why I even bother any more." He sadly mused that his chosen isolation was the only way he thought he could survive the emotional scarring left from being dumped by SnakeMan.

The irony of making his living tailoring special tights for supos wasn't lost on Wes. The very type of people he least wanted to be around now were his bread and butter. But this was the thing he knew how to do best, he was damn good at it, and he had developed several fabrics that had become the standards for supo tights. So, he had to endure fittings with supos several days a week, especially weekends, when their tights tended to get torn, burned, or mutilated by whatever suvil destruction technique a particular supo's arch rival had come up with this time. And holidays were the worst. Seemed suvils worked overtime,

2

wreaking havoc and spreading mayhem on holiday weekends.

He was startled out of his lonely reverie by a loud crash. He wrapped the towel around his waist and dashed down the hall into the den to find a tall, dark and handsome, but kind of scruffy looking man standing inside the large, open window in the center of a pile of rubble, looking embarrassed.

The man looked over at Wes sheepishly and said, "Sorry." He pointed down at the mess. "What was that?"

Wes's temper flared, and he snorted as he pointed angrily at the front door, "Can't you fucking supos ever just knock and come in the fuckin' door like everyone else? It's not like you have to make a grand entrance every time! That Cyberloom was brand new! I don't suppose you can just 'recreate it like new' with your magic powers or something, can you?"

SpanMan looked down guiltily at the rubble and mumbled, "I said I'm sorry. I'll pay for it, whatever it was."

"Pay for it! Pay for it!" Wes threw his hands up and said, "That means I have to wait six weeks for another one, and do you know how hard it is to get anything delivered out here?" He stomped his bare foot and pointed at SpanMan. "Are you gonna have to tell GravelMan, TreeWoman and SlitherBoy why their tights won't be ready for two months at least? No! I'll have to be the one to tell them some klutzy supo destroyed my Cyberloom ... and GravelMan will be shittin' rocks!"

SpanMan waved his hands. "Calm the fuck down, kid! I told you I'm sorry, OK? Jeezus H. Christ! I'll personally go and pick up a new one of these, uh, hyperlooms or whatever, ok? Gimme a break!"

Wes counted to ten to calm his nerves, and when that didn't work, he counted again in Kleptonian, stealing glances at the handsome man with the two-day-old stubble and very blue eyes. Calmly, he asked, "So whatever was your problem?"

"It was my clothes ... well, what's left of them. I was making a final glide toward the window and because of an air gust I had to stretch a part of my body that, unfortunately, caused this brutal wedgie, and I got real distracted, and here I am."

Wes struggled not to smile, but it was too much, and he broke out into the most delighted guffaw he had had in months. "Whoa! You want me to make you a guaranteed wedgie-free suit, right?"

SpanMan affected his trademark sexy grin and nodded his head. "Uh, yeah, OwlMan highly recommended you, and, uh, I need one kinda fast."

Wes went over to his computer and brought up his Spandexign program. "OK, who are you, what do you do, and what are your specific design needs?"

SpanMan puffed out his chest, deepened his voice and proudly proclaimed, "I am SpanMan!"

Wes nodded his head. "And ...?"

SpanMan looked perplexed. He gesticulated and repeated, "I am SpanMan," a little less bravado in his tone.

"I got that. So what do you do? What do you need in a suit?"

SpanMan shook his head in disbelief. "Wait ... You don't know who I am? You don't ...?"

Wes shook his head and said with a hint of sarcasm, "Uh, no, big guy, sorry. I've never heard of you, so you have to tell me what you need."

His voice took on a whiny tone, "But I'm all over the news! I get more face-time than 78% of the state-accredited supos! Last year, I was number six on the most popular supo list on Perilopolis News Channel 3! I made number twenty-four in the Super Who's Who Hall of Fame Edition! You can't tell me you've never heard of me! Here," he reached over to a bag and snatched the contents out, unfurling a less damaged suit. "Maybe you just need to see me in my tights to jog your memory! But I haven't shaved today, and I need a haircut, so ..."

He held the blue tights with the SpanMan logo in front of himself as Wes shook his head apologetically. "Sorry, I don't recognize you. If you would just tell me what you do ..."

"I ... I ..." he was flustered and at a loss for words. "Don't you watch the news?"

"No. I don't watch the news, and I don't read the papers or any of that stuff. Look, I'm sorry, I'm just not into supos and suvils and all that drama. And with so many supos from all the big cities, Calamityville, Villaintown, Disastro City, everywhere, coming up here, I can't keep track of all you guys." He smiled warmly at the man and said nicely, "But I'll make you a fine suit, if you'll tell me what you need."

SpanMan looked defeated, a new experience for him. He mumbled, "Whatever."

Wes tried to be patient. "Let me see the suit." He took it and said, "I see this is Supospandex. You need a lot of expansion in your material?"

SpanMan rolled his eyes and affected some sarcasm of his own, "Well, ye ... eah. SpanMan? You know, ex-S-P-A-N-d-i-n-g Man?" He stretched both of his hands to the respective far walls and brought them back with a zipping sound, then made his right arm bulk up to the size of a beer keg, ripping his shirt sleeve, and shrunk it just as fast. "I can make my body do anything, and I have a lot of strength, even when I'm stretched out flying."

Wes arched his eyebrows and nodded approvingly, just because he knew the guy really needed his ego stroked. He couldn't care less, although he did briefly picture the guy's cock expanding and lengthening in his – but this was business, and it didn't matter how hot the guy looked, he would not entertain any lustful thoughts for any supo, not after SnakeMan. No, he would never even consider thinking sexually of another supo. Never, never, never.

"OK, I need to know what the limits of your expansion are, if you know them, and I need to know what your arch enemies usually fight you with, like ray-guns, light-sabers, bullets, bombs, or fire, ice, magnetics, that kind of thing."

The supo considered all that and said, "Well, I think my length limit is about forty feet per limb." He held his hand at regular arm's length, peered down to the tips of his fingers, and then shot his arm out the open window, narrowly missing the trunk and a lower branch of a 136-year-old knotty pine, startling three doves enough for one to leave a bird dropping that stretched all the way down his arm as he extended it. His face wrinkled with distaste, and he quickly retracted his limb, wiping it off with a non-wedgie part of his torn pants, muttering something about those fucking birds.

He looked back at Wes and said, "My arch enemy is BondageMan. He spins rope out his wrists, and that rope is the only thing known that can contain me. I have to wrap him completely with my stretched body to contain him ... and I have to be *really* careful exactly what I wrap around what; the first time I had him wholly contained, he bit me in the balls and escaped when I snapped back to normal size, screaming. He's a devious fucker, not to mention deviant. But there's a couple of other suvils I have to deal with." He went on to explain the few weapons that had ever given him any trouble and how he had fought them.

When he finished, Wes said, "Alrighty then. Now, we just need some measurements. Strip."

SpanMan stammered, "N-n-naked?"

Wes rolled his eyes. "Just to your underwear."

"I'm not wearing underwear."

Wes arched his eyebrows again and drolled, "Well then, naked it is."

SpanMan started unbuttoning his shirt, but eyed Wes suspiciously. "You're not, you know ... light in the loafers, are you?"

"Excuse me?" Wes retorted.

"You know," he flapped his wrists and minced a little. "A pole dancer? Butt muncher? Pillow biter?"

Wes couldn't believe his ears. He was torn between busting out laughing and lashing out indignantly. He took a moment to compose himself and replied, "As you said earlier: Jeezus H. Christ! I'm your tailor! But I guess I really don't want to be your tailor. Why don't you just leave?" He shut his computer off, stood up and pointed at the window.

"Whoa, whoa, whoa! I'm sorry! I'm sorry! No need to get all mad or anything. I'm getting naked, see? You can take your measurements and do whatever you do. It's all good, just calm down. I didn't mean anything by it," he babbled as he shucked his tights off. "Look, I really need this suit bad. I'm sorry if I offended you, OK? I'm just uncomfortable with ..."

"With gays. Fags. Queers," Wes finished for him. "Well I am a queer, Mr. SpanMan. Think you can handle that?" He leered. "I'm sure you're aware that supo tights, especially the type you need, are exponentially more complicated than regular clothes. I'm going to be touching your body and feeling around. If you can't handle that, then put your clothes back on and get the hell out of my house."

SpanMan put his hands up placatingly. "No, no, I'm sorry! Really! It's no problem! See? I'm naked! It's OK! I don't care if you're, you know ..."

Wes shook his head with disgust and said, "I really don't need this. You should leave. I do not want to make your suit. Goodbye, Mr. SpanMan. Out the window."

"No, please! Please? I haven't had a good suit in years! It's so embarrassing being interviewed at a disaster or fight scene in tights that are sagging off or torn to shreds! A couple of months ago I was on national news with half my suit torn off! I still can't review that interview more than once a week. I don't care what you do. Touch me all you want. You can even touch my privates. Here, touch me, I don't care." He stepped over to Wes and jutted his groin forward, which actually just irritated Wes even more – even if he did have a really impressive cock, hanging soft about five or six thick inches over big furry orbs.

The man was a stud, no doubt about it. Wes could eye measurements accurately at forty paces, and this stud was perfectly proportioned, including there – but then all those damn super heroes were pretty spectacular, weren't they? This one had the proverbial square jaw and aquiline nose, and when he smiled, well, you could almost overlook the arrested emotional development. Being a superhero didn't automatically make you smart or socially viable; it just meant you had some extraordinary capability, and with it, you either went supo or suvil. There were more suvils, though because they could make fortunes being Supervillains, whereas supos just got a steady paycheck, gated condominium housing, and a pretty decent 401K from The League.

He looked up and noticed SpanMan had a dusting of chest hair that poured down a funnel shaped treasure trail ending in a neatly trimmed bush above his ample equipment. Moderate male body hair turned Wes on, and it was always nice to get a reminder when seeing supos naked that, though they had some kind of powers, they were after all, still human (well, maybe except for that Mr. Chernobyl) – but he refused to care or be interested.

Wes thought about it for a long moment as SpanMan displayed himself with a pleading look. He finally frowned and said, "Against my better judgment ... I guess ... OK."

SpanMan released the breath he'd been holding and said, "Thanks, kid, I really appreciate it. Do what ya gotta do."

Wes pulled his trusty bodymeter out of his desk and got started. SpanMan was cool, but when Wes wrapped the bodymeter around his genitals, SpanMan shuddered and giggled. He looked down at the tailor and teased, "You need me to get hard, or expand it?" His cock jerked and started filling out as he spoke.

"No. Do not get hard. Do not expand. Do not talk."

The supo hmmphed and said, "You're no fun." But, his cock continued to grow.

Wes stopped and looked up. "I said, do not get hard."

8

"I can't help it if it gets hard when someone's feeling all over it! Whattaya expect?"

Wes tipped one corner of his mouth up and the other down. "I wouldn't expect your dick to respond to a queer's touch."

SpanMan shuffled around nervously and mumbled, "Well … Shit, man … He don't know who's touching him. As far as he knows, you could be a woman. I'm not turned on by you touching me there, y'know."

However, his cock was standing perpendicular to his body by the time he finished saying that. Wes looked up at him and rolled his eyes. "Well touching 'him' does nothing for me, either, so … maybe you need a time out?" he asked in a mildly snide tone.

SpanMan looked down at him almost indignantly. "Really? Touching my dick don't do anything for you?" He didn't give Wes time to answer. "I mean, I'm pretty well hung, as you can see, and it's a pretty nice looking package." He cocked his head imploringly. "You don't get anything from touching it?"

Wes shook his head and displayed a bored expression as he sat back on his heels. He didn't even need to measure the supo's genitals; he'd done it just to mess with the guy's head and make him squirm. Apparently, the supo was too dense to recall that no previous tailor had ever had to measure his cock to get a fit.

"But," he pointed down at his magnificent erection and said, "This is one hell of a dick! Wouldn't you say this is a perfect specimen of male anatomy? It's nearly ten inches when it's hard … and that's without 'expanding' it! I can make it fucking humongous, if I want!"

Wes retorted, "All you straight guys think gay guys just automatically drool over every male we see! Do you drool over every single woman you see, just cuz she's female?"

He cocked his head, perplexed. "Well, no. Ugly or fat broads don't do nothin' for me, but …"

Wes interjected incredulously, "Broads? Did you just use the term broads?"

SpanMan ignored that and stuck with his line of thought. "But I'm not a dog! I'm like, the perfect male! I also make the top twenty sexiest supos list every fucking year! How can you not be turned on by me?"

Wes looked up past the huge erection to his face and tried to think of a different sign of rejection than rolling his eyes. He spread his knees wide on the floor and hunkered his pelvis up for view, still covered in only a towel wrapped around his waist. He pointed down at his own groin with both hands and said, "Nothing, see? Nada. You don't do a thing for me." A smug little smile graced his face.

Feeling his ego and his manhood insulted, he retorted, "Well how about this?" He expanded his cock and balls rapidly. The already prodigious member shot out to about three feet in length and attained a circumference of about one and a half feet. His balls became the size of cantaloupes. It really looked rather absurd, but surprisingly didn't seem to affect the supo's balance.

Well, it was kind of fascinating to see a cock that huge, up close, and the scent was powerful, being right in front of his nose. Male groin scent was heavenly to Wes, and SpanMan's scent was musky, tart, and very appealing.

"Aha!" He startled Wes out of his observation. Wes looked at SpanMan's finger pointing down at his towel and saw, much to his chagrin, that it was tenting. "I knew you couldn't really not be hot for it!" He rolled his hips back and forth suggestively and grinned, all cocky and smug.

Wes blushed and shook his head to clear it. He stammered, "W-w-well, so what? You just put a huge cock and balls in front of my face! I've never seen anything like that in my life. As long as I wasn't noticing you, and just saw a big dick, then, well ..."

SpanMan let his genitals shrink back to normal. He watched Wes's towel sink back down into his lap, and his own cock sagged and drooped as well. Then he sounded almost like his feelings got hurt when he supposed, "You really don't like me, do you?"

Wes looked up at him, raised an eyebrow and snorted, "Whatever gave you that idea?"

"Look, I know we got off on the wrong foot and all, but I'm really a nice guy, once you get to know ..."

Wes cut him off, "What? A nice guy? I've known you less than an hour, and you've insulted me several times. You're a homophobe, a misogynist; you're massively insecure, vain, and apparently not as sharp as you like to think you are ... what's not to like?"

The butch supo's lower lip actually quivered for a moment there, and he deflated. He stepped – or staggered – backward to a chair and sat down, looking deeply contemplative, even pouting. He looked more appealing to Wes now. After a long silence, he muttered under his breath, "I'm not stupid." He glanced up and continued, "I may not be the smartest supo out there, but ... I'm not stupid."

Wes mumbled, "I didn't call you stupid."

"Yes, you did. Look, I know I'm not the sharpest tool in the shed, but hey, I get by." He stared at the floor for a minute in awkward silence, then looked back up at Wes. "So ... are you saying you would be attracted to me if you weren't turned off by my personality?"

Wes reluctantly nodded his head and said, "Well ... maybe. I mean, no one can deny you've got one hell of a body and your face is, well, gorgeous, but ..."

"But?"

"But, I don't do super heroes, so there's no chance of anything happening anyway, even if you weren't an asshole."

"Why don't you do super heroes? Most people dream of getting with a supo. We have groupies out the ying yang."

Wes sounded melancholy, "Well, not this one. I wouldn't touch a supo with a borrowed tongue."

"What happened to you?" He rose and stepped over to Wes, kneeling down with a genuinely concerned look on his face. Wes kept his head down. SpanMan hooked his finger under his chin and pulled up gently. "Something bad happened to you. Some supo must have …"

Wes's gut was churning as the memories came welling up and vied for attention with his wonder at how this jerk was all of a sudden being so kind and sympathetic. And he sensed it was genuine. It didn't fit though, so he was trying not to believe it. Wes couldn't understand his sudden need to open up. He had never talked about it to anyone. It had only been the last year when he reached a point where he was even able to take on supo clients again. SnakeMan had destroyed his trust in people, especially supos. He had ripped his heart out and tossed it into a deep pit of despair. Wes had not healed as three years had dragged by, with so very many days when he seriously wondered if this life was worth bothering with anymore.

SpanMan sat down on the floor next to him, wrapped his arm around him, and kind of leaned into his shoulder. He said softly, "I talk shit a lot, but I'm really not as … as unfeeling or selfish as I come off. I've … been hurt, too. I can tell you've been hurt. I can see it in your eyes, kid. Tell me about it."

Wes glanced over at him and said, "It's Wesley. Wes."

"Wesley. Nice to meet you. So tell me about it."

Wes shook his head and sniffed. "You don't wanna hear some faggot whine about having his heart broken by …" He abruptly stopped and started to stand up. "We're supposed to be fitting you for …"

SpanMan grabbed his arm and pulled him back down gently. "I'm not in a hurry. I want you to see that I'm not an asshole … at least not all the time." He smirked, so did Wes.

Wes then scowled and said, "You don't need to prove anything to me, SpanMan. And I know you don't want to hear my troubles. Let's just keep this professional, OK?" He started to stand again.

SpanMan again kept him from getting up. "Hey, it's a little late to keep this from getting personal, don't ya think? Besides the fact that we're both sitting on the floor in the middle of your den, naked …" He grinned, then got serious again. "I wanna hear your story, Wes. Tell me who broke your heart and how he did it. Really, I wanna hear it."

"What makes you think I would tell you my most personal and painful feelings and experiences? I just met you a little while ago ... and we haven't exactly bonded. I'm not so pathetic that I need to go around telling every jerkoff supo that comes along my story." He saw the flinch in SpanMan's cheek and realized that, unlike just a couple of minutes ago, he felt bad about insulting him now. He didn't know what to think of that. He smiled wanly at him and said in a nice tone, "Sorry. But you are, y'know ... a jerkoff."

SpanMan nodded and said, "Yeah. I am. I know that, but it's ... a girlfriend once told me that all this shit I say is just a defense mechanism, like to cover for being such a softy. I don't ... I really don't like anyone thinking I'm soft. I guess I say shit to make sure no one will think I'm, you know ... weak or something."

Wes had to snap his jaw shut to keep from showing how stunned he was at this macho supo opening up and admitting his vulnerabilities to him. They'd just met, and their interactions had mostly just been contentious. This was so unreal, but it was intriguing, and he was feeling some kind of connection growing between them minute-by-minute. He didn't understand it, but for some reason, he wasn't inclined to fight it, or even try to figure it out.

He was only able to say, "Being nice and sharing emotion isn't weakness, SpanMan. That you can be kind, and have your heart broken, doesn't mean you're weak; it means you're human."

SpanMan narrowed his eyes, and a certain sadness showed in them. "I'm not human; I'm a freak, Wes. That's why I live in League City with the other freaks. You guys call us superheroes, but we're all just freaks. I only know of a handful of supos who have any kind of real love in their lives. The general population can't handle thinking of us as real flesh and blood people. Even we refer to the genpop as 'humans' most of the time, so what does that make us? We're not immortal, well mostly, and we're not from outer space, mostly. But they won't let us feel normal in any way. And love? Well, that's ... that's not for us, as far as the genpop are concerned. They don't want their superheroes to love. When you love, you're ... vulnerable."

Wes shook his head in awe and sympathy. There was another long silence while they just looked into each other's eyes. Finally, Wes broke the silence, "It's not weakness, Span, it's ... it's a basic need. How lonely would it be never to feel love? How lonely would it be not even to try for it, to just accept that you can't have it?"

SpanMan took a bit to respond, then said just above a whisper, "You tell me. How lonely is it, Wesley?"

Wes dropped his gaze to their knees and blushed. Tears came to his eyes and threatened to spill out. He felt movement at his shoulder and then warm breath on the side of his face. His breath hitched, and he didn't dare move a muscle. Then he felt lips on his cheek. He tried to suppress the instinctive response of jerking away from any contact – especially from a supo, and one whom he thought of as a homophobe. He managed instead to slowly turn his head to face this handsome jerk, who all of a sudden had shown himself to be just as human, lonely and vulnerable as he was.

The supo leaned down and kissed him feather lightly on the lips. SpanMan's surprise at his own actions was diminished when he drew back to watch Wes's reaction. The kid looked stunned, but he could see the wonder and uncertainty, the hope and the need in Wes's eyes. He kept asking himself why he was finally letting himself go with his desires after all these years, with this young naked tailor who said he didn't even like him but seemed to be responding to his pass. He smiled at Wes and brought his hand around to cup the back of his head and pull him into a more lingering kiss.

A little whimpering moan escaped Wes's throat, and he relaxed into SpanMan's hold, kissing back with growing passion. His arm went up around SpanMan's neck as the supo pulled his smaller body practically into his lap, losing the towel in the process. After a passionate couple of minutes, Wes broke the kiss and drew his head back, breathing hard. "What's your given name, when you're not on duty?"

SpanMan grinned widely. "Kelso. Kelso Allard."

"Mmmm, I like that. It's kind of different. Kelso. I like that." He cocked his head and said, "What are we doing? I thought you didn't like queers?"

Kelso nuzzled into Wes's neck and mumbled as he inhaled his scent, "Aww hell, baby, ain't you figured out I'm mostly full of shit? I've been hidin' in the closet so long I almost forgot how hot a cute thing like you can get me." He licked and nibbled his way down Wes's torso and paused, breathing raggedly over his navel. "Seriously, I've been denying myself for years, and you just ... made me ... I don't know why I'm ..." He gave up trying to explain, lifted Wes's middle up, dipped his head and just swallowed Wes's dripping cock whole. Wes moaned loudly and groped underneath for Kelso's cock. He found it and just let it throb in his hand while Kelso worked his magic on him.

Within minutes, Wes got really close to cuming and lifted Kelso's head out of his lap. He panted and said, "I'm too close." Kelso grinned and lunged at his mouth for a kiss, toppling them over, so Wes was on his back as he climbed over him.

He raised up on his hands and knees and gazed down on Wes's prone body. He shook his head and said, "Something about you, from the moment I laid eyes on you ... I don't know what it is, but you threw me off my game the moment I got here."

Wes looked up into his eyes and asked, in all seriousness, just for clarification, "Is this just ... is it just gonna be ... sex? I mean, that would be fine; I really need it, and I don't wanna push you to say something you don't feel or anything, but ... I just wanna know if you're feeling the kind of things I keep feeling about you? I mean, I know we just met, and this is crazy, and you're a jerk, and I'm this pathetic tailor hiding up on a mountain and ..."

They both busted out laughing. Kelso dropped his head onto Wes's chest, and they kept laughing for a good minute or so. Finally, he raised his head back up and gazed into Wes's eyes. "Mmmm-mm. No, baby. It's more than just sex ... which we ain't even had yet!" They chuckled, and he continued, "I don't know. Who can say? Like you said, we just met; we both agreed I'm a jerkoff, and I'm not all that good at this emotional stuff, y'know? But I do know I feel something different, something that ... that let me take off my mask for you, when I only just met you. I keep getting this sense that this was, like, meant to be or something. Hell, you had me naked in ten minutes! Who's in control here, anyway?"

Wes grinned up at him as he reached up, grabbed his dangling erection and started stroking it lovingly. He moaned appreciatively at the perfect cock and said, "You're the supo. So take me already."

Kelso grinned lustily. If there's one thing he liked, it was being the man in control. Wes giving him that signal was all he needed. He leaned down and whispered in his ear, "You ready for me, baby?"

Wes wrapped his legs up around Kelso's hips. "Yes, but it's been so long, and you're so big ..."

Kelso murmured in his ear, "Don't worry, baby, don't you worry about a thing." He spit on his hand and mixed it with his plentiful precum and pushed at the entrance.

They both grunted and moaned as he sank slowly in, kissing him and whispering little things in his ear, working his way down with a tenderness that Wes's only other lover had never shown.

When he bottomed out, he just stayed there for a bit, grinding his hips around, stirring Wes up inside. Wes moaned and panted, writhed around under him and squeezed the cock in his sheath. Kelso started pumping with long, slow strokes. Wes rolled his head from side to side on the floor in ecstasy like he'd never known. "Oh yes, oh yes, oh God, Kelso!" he yelled.

"You like that?"

"Oh God, yes!" He began working his hips up to meet his thrusts. He curled himself up so that he could work his ass and kiss, lick and nibble on Kelso's chest and the hollow at the base of his throat at the same time.

Kelso grunted and moaned as he drove it home for a few minutes. Then he sank it in and stopped. He leaned down and whispered in Wes's ear, "I got somethin' special for ya, baby, somethin' just one other boy from a long time ago and only a few women have experienced. You want it?"

Wes stared into his eyes, looking back and forth, wondering why he automatically wanted to trust this guy. Slowly he nodded his head. He felt something different inside him. Kelso was already big, but he felt him start to grow, thickening and lengthening gradually. Of course! This was Kelso's supo ability – hell, he'd already demonstrated this trick. He then tensed up, wondering if Kelso might get carried away and not know when to stop.

As if reading his mind, Kelso said, "No, I'm not like that supo whose climax blew off the top of his wife's head. The special thing is this – when I'm inside someone's body, if I expand my dick, for some reason, their body will expand with it, as long as my dick don't lose contact totally with their body for more than a few seconds. So, we both expand, and the sensations expand with us. The feeling, the sensitivity, all of it expands. It's really intense, so you need to prepare your mind for it. Get ready, Wesley, I'm gonna fuck you and take you where no one else can."

And he did. As his cock expanded to maybe four times its thickness, Wes felt both his body and his mind expand in perfectly tight proportion to Kelso's cock – and it was almost too intense to bear. He was afraid at times that his mind was just going to dump him into a stir-fry state. He had never even fantasized this level of ecstasy was possible.

It was, and it was possible for at least the two hours they went at it nonstop (a power Kelso hadn't realized he had). And when they took a break just for appearances, Wes had already realized that, whatever particular positions and intersections got expanded, the one thing that never varied from massive was the caring Kelso showed. And despite the different proportions, sizes, or sensations, no matter what Kelso filled, he filled it with love.

And that is what it became, whether tender and romantic or rough and animalistic, it was lovemaking. Over the next few weeks, between Span's bouts with would-be (but not better-dressed) world conquerors, they came to accept their love for each other. After two months, they bought a tesseract condo in Perilopolis, renaming it SpanSpace. His fellow League members very much welcomed the changes in SpanMan. He was no longer the gruff and abrasive asshole he had been for so long – and his ratings went up. He was invited onto all the top rated talk shows, and he even introduced his own line of SpanMan action figures for kids.

And they lived happily ever after in well-tailored, wedgie-free tights.

Flying Fuck
By Jay Starre

Cloud Runner soared over the valley. His slate gray wings spread wide, while his sharp eyes scanned the streams and meadows for his prey. There he was! Cloud Runner grinned triumphantly. He murmured into his phone jack without altering his floating glide.

"On the ground, cruising the nearby highway." His partner received the call and sped toward an interception point.

The escaped convict had abandoned his orange prison uniform, but Cloud Runner's keen eyesight and police work honed intelligence had allowed him to spot the man regardless. General build, hair color, erratic manner of hiking through the woods, all indicated this was their man.

Cloud Runner floated on the updrafts, his body almost immobile in the air now that he had his prey in sight. The man below was unaware of the masked superhero hovering above. Silence was Cloud Runner's key to success. The reverberating chop of a police helicopter or drone of an airplane would have sent the convict scurrying for cover. Now he rested by a stream plainly in Cloud Runner's sight.

Dag, Cloud Runner's partner, had called for backup, and now three police vehicles were closing in on the unsuspecting convict. Cloud Runner waited patiently, rising and falling in gentle arcs, savoring the wind in his hair and on his face. The orange mask he wore covered only the upper half of his face and left a mop of yellow-gold hair revealed to ruffle in the breeze.

Cloud Runner transmitted directions to the half dozen armed police while the convict actually snoozed complacently beside a mountain stream he'd chosen as his hideaway. Cloud Runner had immediately picked out Dag, the stealthy but powerful stride and the blaze of red hair familiar and appreciated by the masked superhero.

Cloud Runner's cock stirred under the skin-tight black bodysuit of his costume. The apprehension of prey, and the sight of his muscular young partner about to do just that, stirred his sexual senses. The joy of flight always thrilled Cloud Runner, and his cock was often semi-hard throughout his airborne journeys.

But it was seeing Dag, or thinking of Dag, that stiffened the superhero's cock into a full-blown erection. With that raging hard-on pulsing under his costume, Cloud Runner continued to whisper instructions into his radio jack while the police followed his exact directions.

He laughed out loud when the surprised convict leaped to his feet, too late to do anything but throw up his hands in surrender. From below, the six officers who made the capture looked up toward the sky and waved.

Dag's red hair blazed in the sunlight as he waved vigorously along with the others. Cloud Runner made a looping fly-by in response, his wide gray wingspan of fabricated feathers fluttering in the wind. He soared off, his cock still hard and his balls full of unspent spew. He would have to return to his airy hideaway and blow a load by hand! The pent-up tension was too much.

Dag called in half an hour later to report the convict was back at the station under lock and key. "Great job once again, Cloud. What about that complementary flight you've been promising me? Won't you take me for a spin up in the skies?"

The voice was light and teasing as Dag called the superhero by his shortened name. Only Dag called him Cloud, but he didn't object. The redheaded cop was barely twenty-two, ten years younger than Cloud Runner himself. Except for a score of criminals he'd plucked from the earth while they were on the run, Cloud Runner had never taken anyone on a flight in his career as a superhero. No free rides for adoring fans. Or fellow cops.

But Dag was special.

As they chatted over the radio on their own private line, Cloud Runner was semi-naked and lustily flailing his big boner. His black bodysuit was unzipped and wide open to the crotch, his cock out in the open and purple with throbbing need. A gooey dribble of nut-juice continually leaked from the engorged piss slit on the fat crown as Cloud Runner pumped away.

Dag's voice hummed in his ear, soft and sexy. The image of the redhead's muscular frame, broad shoulders, thick thighs and tight bubble-butt, flashed through Cloud Runner's active mind.

"Sure. I'll take you up. How about tomorrow afternoon?" Cloud Runner found himself blurting out, the intensity of his jerk-off session rising toward orgasm, and his usually formidable defenses dangerously diminished. The fantasy of Dag in his arms, in the air, his firm asscheeks beneath Cloud Runner's strong thighs reared up in the superhero's mind.

With a shudder, he blew. An arcing stream of cum rocketed out into the air. Dag laughed on the other end of the phone line, unaware of Cloud Runner's orgasm.

"You've said that before, then backed out at the last minute. Tell you what, superhero, how about if I offer to suck you off? Would my lips wrapped around your hard-on be enough to coerce you into a flying lesson?"

Cloud Runner's thighs splayed wide as he sat back and allowed his cum to spew. Ah, sweet release! Dag's nasty teasing was not unusual, and Cloud Runner grinned at the blatant come-on. In all his years as the masked superhero, flying since he was a teenager, he had never had sex with anyone while in uniform.

But, yes, Dag was special.

There was a hitch, of course. Dag was entirely unaware that Cloud Runner was in real life the young police officer's superior. Bradley Mason, Chief of Metropolitan Police, was the secret identity of the famous Cloud Runner.

The promise had been made, and as Dag reminded Cloud Runner, not for the first time. Would he squirm out of fulfilling that promise again at the last minute? What was holding him back?

Dag was special, and that was the biggest hitch. Dag could be very special in Cloud Runner's life, the life of a secretive superhero, who guarded his privacy as if it were the crown jewels of an empire.

And Chief Bradley Mason had barely spoken a dozen times to Officer Dag Smith. As a normal man, the Chief did not seem to interest Dag.

Removing his costume, Cloud Runner reverted to merely Chief Mason. He wiped up his cum with a towel and laughed at himself. He wasn't going to be able to resist the young redhead this time. He just couldn't help himself, and he knew it. Superhero but not a saint, he had many of the usual human failings. Cloud Runner was in lust with the redheaded cop and had to act on it.

Their rendezvous was typical. It was Dag's duty to contact Cloud Runner when there was some need for his services. He would radio on their private line, and Cloud Runner would answer, although usually he was Chief Mason when he did reply. They would agree to meet somewhere away from prying eyes.

Rarely had the reclusive superhero been spotted in real life, and rarer still, the photographs of him published in newspapers and magazines. His broad wingspan of dark grey wings, vivid orange mask and jet-black bodysuit were seen in the skies by the lucky few, and his unlucky prey, but Cloud Runner never offered interviews to a greedy press.

So the young officer and the superhero met outside of the limits of the sprawling metropolis they both served. Officer Dag drove his police cruiser while Cloud Runner cruised the skies, alighting with wings spread dramatically on the isolated hilltop they had agreed on as the rendezvous point.

Dag laughed out loud when the superhero dropped down from the heavens at his feet. "I have to confess, Cloud, I've had dreams of flying since I was just a little boy. Is it really going to come true today? Or will you give me some bullshit excuse again?"

Those particular words couldn't have been chosen more perfectly. Cloud Runner almost gasped as the impact of Dag's statement hit home. The superhero's deepest secret had just been blurted out by this unsuspecting young police officer.

Bradley Mason had dreamed of flying as a boy, too. Incessantly.

Night after night, as a child he took flight. He would start off running in a field. Then he would spread his arms, and after enormous effort, his little thighs pumping, rise into the air, triumphantly. Or, he would perch on a hilltop then run down the slope full speed until once more, his effort would pay off, and he would rise, soaring into the skies, free and ecstatic and flying.

On awakening, Bradley Mason would experience the keenest disappointment. But he would also recall with almost perfect memory that tantalizing experience of flight – even though it had merely been a dream.

When his sixteenth birthday arrived, something unaccountable happened.

He had sought out hill tops often as a boy and teenager. The windswept openness called to him. He ached to soar into the heavens, free of the bonds of the earth. On his birthday, lightning struck him. A bolt of electric energy seared through his core as he ran down the slope, his arms waving, his heart already soaring. He lifted off.

For hours that afternoon, the young Bradley Mason soared over hills and dales. He was absolutely certain it was all a dream, until he reluctantly landed and realized he wasn't going to wake up. He could fly!

He never understood it, some kind of mental and physical melding of supreme willpower had combined in him, he supposed, when lightning struck him. In any case, he had kept the ability a secret, then after joining the police force as a young man, he donned the costume of the Cloud Runner and became a superhero.

Cloud Runner had materialized in his mysterious uniform only five years previously. Now, here he was, about to share his precious gift of flight with someone else. Dag's eager green eyes danced with nervous expectation as he stared up at Cloud Runner perched on the lee of the slope above him.

Cloud Runner laughed out loud, surrendering to his desire. With a wicked grin between plump lips, he raised his arms and spread his wings, silver and jet feathers arcing above his black-suited body.

"Run down the slope, Dag! Run like you can fly!"

Dag whooped as he whirled and followed Cloud Runner's instructions. They had been partners in action for over a year, and Dag trusted his flying superbuddy. His muscular thighs pumped as they raced down the open hillside.

Cloud Runner rose effortlessly, his arms out as he began to speed toward the racing cop. It only took a few seconds, during which Cloud Runner banished any last minute doubts, for the superhero to reach the cop.

Cloud Runner plucked Dag off the ground and soared upwards.

"Oh my god! Fuck! Oh my god!" Dag shrieked. His arms and legs flailed as he dangled from Cloud Runner's strong arms with the ground careening away in a sickening drop.

Cloud Runner had scooped Dag up from under his armpits, but the superhero planned to offer Dag more than just a dangling kite ride. Dag would fly with Cloud Runner, truly fly with him.

"Relax, Dag. Feel the air racing over us. Feel it under us, feel it holding us up. Float with me. Fly with me."

The shouted commands focused Dag's adrenalin-muddled thoughts. With a deep inhale, Dag spread his own arms and faced the direction they flew, rather than staring downwards in a terrified glare.

It was almost instantaneous. A cushion of flowing air slid under his body, lifting his chest, his belly, his hips, and finally his thrashing thighs. Dag felt tears stinging his eyes. He was flying!

"Good job, Dag. Relax and trust me. We're going for a ride."

Dag beamed from ear to ear, regardless of the few tears leaking from the corners of his eyes and streaking away in the wind. They were going fast! How fast? For the next few moments, Dag merely allowed himself to truly release into Cloud Runner's embrace, feeling his own body rise up on that cushion of air and slowly meld into the flying superhero above him.

The air was warm on that summer afternoon, but eddying currents blew cooler across them, and suddenly Dag was aware of more than the fact he was flying. Cloud Runner's body felt hot against his. Dag had floated up to press into the superhero above him, their bodies mashed together in a total embrace.

Dag felt Cloud Runner's big chest pressing into his back. He was sure he felt the pounding of the superhero's heart! Dag's legs had risen to sprawl against Cloud Runner's. The heat of the superhero's thighs pulsed into Dag's hamstrings and calves. Dag's ass mashed into Cloud Runner's crotch. A swollen cock surged against his ass crack. A titillating thrill rocketed through Dag as he realized the superhero had a boner, and it was pressing into Dag's own ass!

Dag's gaze dropped to the far-off earth, and he gasped with shock. They were so high! Treetops were wicked points far below. Streams were like lines on a map, glittering blue-gold in the brilliant sunshine.

"I'm flying. Fuck, Cloud! I'm really flying! I love you!"

Dag shouted that out, his ass wriggling with his effort, up into the twitching boner thrusting out from his superbuddy's hot crotch. He hardly realized what he said and couldn't have cared less that he'd finally admitted his own secret passion.

Dag had fallen hopelessly in love with the mysterious superhero the instant they met.

Cloud Runner heard what Dag said. His heart skipped a beat before he slowly slid his hands out from Dag's armpits along his bulging biceps, along his forearms and finally to drape them outspread, their fingers entwined. He no longer needed to hold up the enraptured cop. They flew together.

Once their fingers were enmeshed, their aerial dance began. With his ebony-silver wings rippling in the wind, Cloud Runner led them on a soaring adventure of discovery. It was late afternoon when they took off, and the sun was already heading toward the western horizon. Cloud Runner flew directly into it, away from the metropolis and prying eyes. They would be alone.

"Listen, Dag," Cloud Runner said in Dag's ear.

Dag cocked his ears. "To what?"

"To nothing."

Dag realized it then. The only sound was the rippling of the air around them. The city sounds were far behind. The forest was far below. Other aerial creatures kept their distance. They were alone in blessed silence.

Cloud Runner's hot body embraced his from above. Every moment of that glorious flight, Dag was alive with sensation. The dizzying view, the sense of floating free from the bonds of earth, and the sense of that heated body throbbing above him, his own rising to press against it, and that stiff cock lying pressed into his ass crack.

Cloud Runner had enjoyed countless hours soaring through the skies. He knew his way around the currents and eddying flows, and he could use them or discard them, his own willpower the real wings of his flight. He spun them around with Dag laughing hysterically in a dizzying twirl and dive, then abruptly reversed direction and soared upwards like an ascending rocket.

The silver wings alternated between spreading wide and then dropping down to envelop Dag beneath. Cloud Runner's hands came down, too, and wrapped tightly around the cop's solid body. The moment when their wild flight transformed into something more wasn't easy to pinpoint, but soon Dag was writhing his lush butt cheeks against the stiff boner thrusting back to meet them.

"I want to be naked! I want to fly naked!"

Dag's thrilled shout had Cloud Runner laughing and equally exhilarated. Dag, the redheaded stud cop was going to be naked in his arms! Cloud Runner swerved in a sharp right angle and dove. "Start stripping. We'll drop off your clothes in that clearing. We can get them later."

"Fuck my clothes. I don't care if we ever get them back," Dag answered with a shout. He was already tearing at his belt with his hands.

As they dove toward the small clearing, trees rose up to meet them. Dag's face froze in a rictus of fright, even though he trusted Cloud Runner entirely. He was frantically pushing down his jeans and underwear as they swooped over the treetops and came over the meadow.

"Like dropping a bomb," Dag shouted gleefully. His pants and underwear floated down into the grass.

"Next run, your shirt and shoes."

Dag shivered, not from cold, but from the delicious sensation of feeling all that wind against his naked crotch, his dangling nads and stiff cock. He spread his thighs wide in a sprawling glide as Cloud Runner lifted them skyward and swerved around for a second run at the meadow.

Blue sky arced above them, then emerald forest appeared, and they were racing toward the ground. Dag unbuttoned his shirt, tearing some of the buttons in his haste, and wiggled out of it just in time. The discarded cloth fluttered in the wind just as he kicked off his shoes.

With thighs wide open, his butt crack was, too. That stiff dick above him throbbed between the cheeks, pressing into him. Dag bit his lip and shouted out loud. "I'm flying! Fuck me while I'm flying!"

Totally naked, other than his socks, Dag sprawled out beneath his protector. He had never felt so wide open. His asshole convulsed with expectation. Air swirled around and through his naked limbs, rubbing sensually over his balls and drooling cock. Air swirled up between his spread thighs and into his ass crack. He began to hump up into Cloud Runner with lewd greed.

"Fuck me, Cloud! Fuck me good!"

Cloud Runner was flying as high on adrenalin as his cop partner. The feel of that naked body beneath him was potently erotic. Their enmeshed bodies soaring over the earth together was an emotionally cathartic experience. His own pent-up need and desire for this sexy young cop burst out of his deepest and most guarded places in his soul.

It was Dag who reached up and between them to tear open Cloud Runner's uniform zipper. The redhead shouted out loud as throbbing boner sprang free, and he felt it in his hands. Cloud Runner reacted instantaneously, his emotions soaring with their sudden ascent. He took them straight up as he pulled Dag's hands out again to spread them wide with his wings. Cloud Runner's naked cock thrust into Dag's writhing butt crack.

Hot flesh met hot flesh. As they rocketed upwards, cock invaded deep crack, shoving and searching until the engorged crown met pulsing sphincter. As they both shouted out loud, that fat helmet tunneled its way into Dag's aching asshole.

"I'm fucked!"

The shriek wafted away in the air racing past their ears. Cloud Runner's entire body throbbed in perfect time to the pulsing of his buried cock. Dag's innards seared him. The young cop's writhing ass pumped naked against his crotch. Cloud Runner shouted out along with his moaning buddy and arced toward the zenith of their upward flight. For a moment as they leveled out, it seemed as if they floated weightlessly, cock embedded in ass, before Cloud Runner began to descend.

In graceful arcs, dancing through the open skies, Cloud Runner fucked his cop buddy. Sweat and pre-cum lubed the piston-prodding prick, while Dag's own desire created a suction in that anal pit that drew Cloud Runner's steaming meat in with relentless greed.

Dag was naked, flying through the air, in the arms of the man he adored. Cock reamed his willing ass. The pounding ache in his guts thrilled his prostate and his balls and his own stiff prick. His cock dribbled a constant spray that rained away from them in glistening droplets. His body floated on a cushion of willpower, uplifted by some unfathomable melding of Cloud Runner's super powers. They twisted, turned, ascended and dove while that cock pumped his ass.

Cloud Runner spread his wings wide and thrust into the heated ass beneath him. Dag's hefty, smooth butt cheeks wiggled in sweaty need against him. The hole clamped over his cock like a hungry vice. The orange-masked superhero dropped his wings when they descended, wrapping them around his partner, roaming his hands over that naked body. He felt the muscular chest, tweaked sensitive nipples, dove farther with his hands across rippled abs and then seized the dripping dick and rubbed it insistently.

Wind caressed them as they soared together locked in their sex-dance. Cloud Runner's hands stroked every part of the naked cop beneath him, while Dag shuddered and moaned between shouts of absolute rapture. Dizzying descents alternated with rocketing ascents, floating glides, and then twisting, bobbing aerial dances.

Cock throbbed hot inside churning bowels. Thrust and withdrawal grew more intense. Eventually, they hovered, the wind merely a rustling breath undulating over their locked bodies.

The sun was behind them, billowing clouds flushed pink before them. Dag's thighs sprawled wide, floating, his ass wide open, too, and his arms spread under Cloud Runner's wings. Cock impaled him, drilling into his guts with peremptory heat. He ground his own muscular butt globes back into that stiff pole, and felt his own purple shaft swell to its limits.

"I'm going to blow! Fuck! I'm going to shoot a load with your cock up my ass!"

The shriek blew away in the silence of the heavens as Dag's cock suddenly erupted. No hand touched it. The twitching crown sprayed a sudden geyser of goo. Dag moaned incoherently as his entire naked body jerked into Cloud Runner's

Cloud Runner laughed out loud as he watched Dag's seed rain down. The cop's tender butt hole clamped and seized Cloud Runner's thrusting dick. Cloud Runner slammed deep, urging all of the young redhead's juice out of his roiling nuts. The squirming, naked ass cheeks against him proved too much. Cloud Runner pulled out just in time to cream Dag's pale ass crack with a load of his own.

"You're cumming, too! Awesome! I'm so in love with you!"

Dag's repeated declaration of love could not be ignored. As Cloud Runner gasped through his orgasm, he began to glide downwards in a gentle swirl, their sweating bodies still entwined as both men released the last of their seed. He was totally satisfied, totally happy.

But was he totally in love?

Cloud Runner felt the wind sweep away the shredded tatters of his resistance. Dag had given his all. What kind of superhero was he to be so afraid?

"I love you, too."

They floated for another hour in companionable silence as the pink sunset became first magenta then darkness. It was in the pale light of a crescent moon they found the clearing where Dag's clothing had been discarded.

When they alighted, Dag moaned out loud, nearly exhausted with the power of the experience. Naked, he turned and embraced his new lover.

Cloud Runner kissed the naked young cop. But he didn't remove his mask. Dag didn't ask him to either, not that evening. Not yet.

Maybe soon. For now, they held each other and sighed. No previous experience in either of their lives compared to what just happened.

A flying fuck. Unbelievable.

Heroes In Waiting
By Troy Storm

The magnificently muscled body stirred on the king-sized bed, stretching and yawning, as a beatific smile spread over his handsome face.

Luxuriant lashes slowly pulled apart and blinked lazily as the god-like form's awareness drifted up from a deep and delicious sleep to an even more delicious waking. Looking down, his gaze traveled over the twin mounds of his solid, chiseled pecs, their stiff nipples rosy and pink in the flush of the new day, bracketing the almost-obscured flat ripple of the retreating swells of his six-pack abs.

Hovering over his crotch, a familiar tangle of dark curls busily bobbed up and down over the funnel of focused wet heat that flooded his midsection, the boiling in his midsection rising in intensity with every determined plunge. Strong young hands pushed underneath to knead the awakening man's powerful butt cheeks.

His heroic dick, morning hard and blow-job bloated, shoved even further down the gulping throat.

What a fucking fantastic way for a loser set of superheroes to begin another bummer of a day, the recipient of the morning treat thought dreamily, pressing his powerful hips up to aid in sinking his super shaft deep in Junior's gut.

Junior gagged and coughed, but before he was forced to jerk his head up to grab a lungful of air, the super staff was able to sink itself into the guzzling maw a treasured inch or two further.

"You'll make it one of these days, sweet lips." The owner of the beef pole gently stroked the damp cheeks of his younger companion. At least, he thought, Junior's got a goal to help him get through the boring days they faced. "And you know you can make me blow a load by just kissing the head of my bone." The young stud could make him blow a load by kissing practically any part of his super body.

"I can make you cum by waggling my tongue at you, old sot," Junior grinned, demonstrating.

The handsome old sex sot grabbed the tousled head and pulled it to his hungry mouth. Locking face and battling tongues, their naked super heroic bodies rolled and thrashed together on the bed. Eventually, licking and tasting, more calm, they fumbled for each other's dicks and slowly jacked each other off, knowing the response of each other so well that at the familiar orgasmic grunt and shiver of imminent expulsion they could whip down and guzzle the morning protein shots without losing a drop.

That way, they hadn't had to wash the sheets for two weeks.

Over cold cereal at the breakfast counter in the kitchen, the old sot and the young hot munched quietly away.

"Sen, what are we going to do today?" asked Junior.

The senior member of the duo sighed. "Same as always, little bud. Wait. Be ready."

"They're never going to call us, are they?" Junior piloted his SooperDooper Hero spoon through the flotilla of sodden whole-wheat squares floating in the bowl of non-fat milk.

"Don't mope, keep the hope," Senior sang brightly. He slid off the high stool and waggled his hips causing his long soft dong to ding smartly from thigh to thigh. "Let's go downstairs and hit the weights early. I'll fuck you on the incline bench if you break 200." He flapped his meat at his young grinning cohort.

"You'll fuck me if I don't break 20."

"Ah, there are no more surprises between this old couple," Senior shrugged, as they started toward the basement stairs, arm in arm. "What we need is something new and …"

An ear-splitting screech of brakes and the sickening crunch of tearing metal stopped the two men in their tracks. Senior dashed for the door.

"Sen, you're naked!"

The older man looked around and grabbed a dishtowel. Clutching it around his waist he shot through the front door as Junior hopped after him pulling on sweat shorts.

An SUV and a package delivery truck were in a shattered heap in the middle of the street; the SUV nearly totaled. The smell of diesel fuel and gasoline filled the air. Neighbors dashed out of their houses, but seeing the two near-naked men running toward the twisted metal, stood back.

Holding the dishtowel around his hips with one hand, Senior looked through the broken window of the crumpled utility vehicle at the stunned young women inside. Junior leaped through the open doorway of the delivery truck to puncture the deployed air bag with one fist and rip the restraining seat belt from around the unconscious deliveryman.

A rush of heated air was followed by a guttural whoosh as leaking fuel caught fire and flames leaped up around the van.

Senior kicked at the unyielding, crumpled door of the SUV. "Cover your eyes, ladies!" he yelled at the gawking neighbors. Dropping the dishtowel, he used both hands to rip first one door from its frame and then another. He pulled three young hysterical, bleeding women out of the wreck and carried them to a far lawn, where he kissed them gently on the forehead and laid them in the grass as they slowly collapsed.

"Thanks, Maude," he said to an older woman hurrying down from her porch to help.

"My pleasure, big guy." She whistled and winked at his not-so privates. Senior blushed and hurried to grab the dropped dishtowel and help his young co-hort, who had carried the young deliveryman to their porch.

Another ear-splitting bang, and both vehicles burst into flames. Senior and Junior circled the inferno, their cheeks puffed. With mighty blows, they snuffed the raging inferno. The neighbors cheered.

"The cops and a fire truck are coming down the street," a middle-aged man yelled from three houses down. "Thanks, George," Senior yelled back as he and Junior dashed up their porch stairs taking note of the unconscious deliveryman lying in the swing.

"Hot looking dude," Junior remarked with a sigh. They dashed inside.

"Another pretty mess fixed up by the lads in waiting," Senior remarked dryly as he tossed the dishtowel aside and checked their diesel-oil spattered, smoky bodies. "Damn, look at us," he grinned. "We're going to have to shower again." He swept his young cohort into his arms where a giggling Junior squirmed out of his loose sweat shorts as Sen trotted toward the shower room off the kitchen.

In the cozy stall, Junior grabbed Senior's semi-hard and shook it firmly. "Put 'er there, pard. Yep. A fine piece of work by the 'Dynamic...'"

"Uh unh," admonished Senior, soaping up. "Registered phrase."

"Ooo-kay." He thought a moment. "'Damnfine Dyno Duo.' How's that senior member? You want to put your dyno stick in and blow out a hole?" Neatly turning in the small space, he backed onto the older man's rapidly hardening meat, sliding it neatly up his ass.

Senior clutched the young man – his spearing dick deep up Junior's butt – lifting the young man off the floor with each forward thrust of his hips.

"You are such a good mentor." The speared young stud purred contentedly and caught Senior's clutching hands in his, scrubbing them over his smooth, shapely chest and circling them over his nipples to bring the nubs to a fiery heat as Sen fucked his young butt with an intensity that triple-thrummed his young heart.

Swimming up from his euphoria, Junior lifted his head. "What's that?"

"It's the doorbell. Let them ring. We're occupied."

"Somebody's in the hallway"

"What?"

"Well, we never lock the door. Shit, somebody's in the kitchen."

"Hello?" A deep voice sounded. "Are you guys back here?" The deliveryman stuck his head through the open door and pulled the shower curtain back. He stared at the duo, staring back at him, frozen under the pouring water – the older fat-free, massively sculpted man plugged up the receptive rump of the younger smoothly muscled one.

"Oh, uh, hi," the deliveryman blinked groggily, looking the naked men up and down. "Sorry, I ... uh, need to use your phone ... my cell got smashed and ..." He checked the conjoined men more carefully. "Holy shit, you two are totally amazing hunks of beef. How the fuck do you get that kind of build? Man, I work my ass off and ..." He peered lower at the visible section of Sen's proud poker poked up Junior's butt. "Ooooh whee, mother of massiveness, how big is that thing?"

"Look, uh ... Mr. Delivery person," Senior huffed, blinking back the pouring water, "we're like in the middle of something here ..."

"Oh, yeah. Oh, man," the guy put a hand on the bathroom wall to steady himself. "I wouldn't mind having some of that myself. That is one beautiful ass." He leaned in to check and raised a shaky thumb. "Dynamite dick, too."

Junior's dropped jaw closed. His frown erased itself. He smiled. "Thanks. Hey, are you OK?"

"Maybe I had better sit down."

Senior instantly grabbed the woozy man, his prong extracting itself from Junior's butt with a slurpy, wet pop.

In the superhero's arms, the deliveryman grinned foolishly up at his rescuer. "Closer is a hell of a lot better than seeing you guys work from afar. But none of that kissing the forehead stuff." He waggled a finger. "Those people out there didn't remember a thing."

Grabbing a couple of bath towels, Junior followed the dripping pair as Senior dragged the deliveryman to a kitchen chair, sitting him down and shoving his head between his legs while pressing his fingers lightly onto the back of the young man's neck.

"Just take deep breaths and relax. You'll be fine."

"Wowee. I feel better already," the young man's voice came from near the floor. "Are you guys like, government agents or something?"

"Don't talk. Yeah, something like that."

"Hottest damn agents I ever saw," the upside down man chuckled. "Do you always do your good works in the buff?" Lifting his head, he noticed Junior busily mopping up water around the chair. "Great ass and phenomenal basket on the kid. Are you two, like, a couple?"

"You could say that." Senior dried himself, beginning to be annoyed. "Shouldn't you be like making a report or something ... outside?"

The man sat up. "The cops didn't even see me on the porch. You're not like ... superheroes, are you?" He looked around conspiratorially. "I saw you rip off those doors and the both of you blow ... man," he snickered, "What a blowjob! Blew the flames right out."

Senior grabbed the man's head and started to plant a kiss on his forehead. The deliveryman's hand shot out to grab the older man's cock and squeeze firmly.

"Aagh!"

"C'mon, guys, work with me, here," the clutcher begged. "What the fuck's going on? You two look like you're having a hell of a lot more fun blowing and...," with his other hand he reached over to stroke the hovering Junior's half-hard dick affectionately as the startled young man first jerked back and then after a moment moved back into the guy's grip.

"And getting blown," the deliveryman continued. "More fun than I have schlepping packages and having ditzy, non-attentive broads total my transportation." He shook his head disconsolately. "The company is not gonna like that mess." He pulled Junior closer, leaning down, his mouth opening to insert Junior's thickening manhood.

"Wait, just a freakin' minute." Senior pushed the two apart. "You don't need to know anything about ..."

Junior put a restraining hand on his older buddy's puffed chest.

"Sen? What were we saying about something new? Look at him. He's cute. He's built. He's got an up-front attitude and a really hot mouth. Look at those lips, man. He could be fun."

The deliveryman straightened smugly in the chair, spreading his hands and legs wide, presenting himself. "You wanna see more." He kicked off his shoes, stood and stripped.

Sen appraised the naked man, squeezing his chest muscles and pinching his tits. "You could use a little defining."

Junior examined the guy's rigid dick and low-hanging balls. "Looks defined to me, Sen."

The older superhero turned the pleased young man around to examine his butt, drawing his hand firmly through the deep crevice dividing the pair of oval muscle masses. "Yeah, maybe you're right." Three very large superhero middle fingers dug into the guy's asshole. Leaning back on Sen's flaring chest, the delivery guy tilted his head back to smile happily up at the older man.

"I could be a great 'something new' for you guys." He reached back to slide his hand down Sen's front and curl his fingers around Sen's hard meat. "I may not be able to take all of that right away, but I'd sure strain a tonsil trying."

Laughing, Sen and Junior grabbed the man by the shoulders and legs and lugged him between them into the living room where they dumped him on the couch.

"OK," Sen announced. "Fuck time. I get the new ass first. What's your name, beauty butt?"

A worried look crossed the man's good-looking features as he appraised Sen's enormous jutting appendage. "Uh, Marky. I, uh, was named after some old guy in the movies who showed his dick. Except it was a fake. Scarred me for life until I made sure mine wasn't. Fake, that is. Hey, dude, I'm … I'm not sure I can take all that up my ass."

"Believe me, you'll be begging for more before we're through." Sitting on the arm of the couch, Sen spread his massive thighs, his wrist-thick dick curving up dramatically between his tensed abductors. "Come show him, Junior." Junior backed onto the upright pole and pressed his ass down. The pole disappeared.

"Any more questions?" Junior asked, bouncing happily up and down.

Marky grinned, licking his lips and squatted between Junior's legs. Junior's dick disappeared. Coming up for air, Marky looked up at the impaled and ingested young man. "Tell all. I'll be listening. My ears are not plugged. Yet." He went back to sucking.

Junior checked with his older mentor. Sen shrugged and continued bouncing his fuck mate up and down on his dick.

"OK," Junior said, "this is the way it is."

A siren went off. Bells clanged. The trio broke apart, in shock.

"What the fuck?!"

"It's the alarm."

"Well, obviously, but does it have to be so fucking loud?"

"What kind of alarm?"

Junior and Senior scrambled toward a concealed LCD panel. "It's a fire a couple of streets over. Some sort of explosion. Some people are trapped." They dashed toward the back door.

"Naked?" the deliveryman called out.

Dashing back, Senior grabbed the fleece shorts – a bit more fitted on him than on his young buddy – and Junior grabbed the dishtowel – slightly more concealing – and shot out the back door. Marky, the deliveryman, jumped into his uniform shorts – underwearless – and followed as best he could as the two men leaped fences and hedges to get to the burning house.

The fire trucks and police cars were already arriving. Junior and Senior paid their shouted demands to stay back no mind and threw themselves into the flames where their barely-concealing garments were immediately consumed. Marky stood back with the gathering crowd, astonished.

Within seconds, the naked men burst back out, bodies over their shoulders and clutched in their arms. A woman and two unconscious children. Junior dashed back into the flames as Sen delivered the victims to the arriving paramedics. Sen hurried to the firemen and grabbed a spewing hose, dragging it much nearer the flames than the firemen were able to stand. A window exploded, and the front door erupted in steam as Junior emerged from the boiling clouds with a man's body slung over his shoulder.

"I think Daddy was trying to fix the gas line," he muttered.

The crowd cheered as the paramedics collected the man from Junior. The police and firemen rushed to assist as Junior also grabbed a fire hose and dragged it into the inferno. Within minutes, the conflagration was under control. More cheering and thanks from the professionals as they came forward with blankets to cover the heroes.

Much hand-shaking and high-fiving as Junior and Sen went from one to the other planting forehead kisses on the startled men and women. The neighbors gave the two heroes thumbs up and moved in to help the suddenly groggy but quickly recovering professionals.

Clutching their blankets around them, Junior and Sen grabbed Marky and slipped through a singed hedge to return to their own house.

Marky raved. "Can I do that, too? Can I save people and stuff? Can I be one of you guys? Who the fuck are you? How did you get to look like you look? Like ... awesome."

"Working our asses off. Literally," Sen said. "In the basement gym. Every day. We gotta be ready. C'mon, we'll show you."

Downstairs, the junior and senior hero in waiting worked phenomenally, pushing the array of muscle-building machines to their limits, while the earnest deliveryman gave a fine showing.

"Well," Junior noted after the work-out, checking Marky's muscular build and muscular crotch. "Maybe you could stick around. What do you think, Sen?"

Sen grinned and turned away, bending over to grab a metal bar, presenting his fine bare butt. "I am Number One," he said. "Forty and fucked by the League. How old are you?"

"Uh, thirty-two," Marky answered, eyes wide on the moist, winking hero's hole.

"Yeah, that makes you the middle guy, Number Two." Junior indicated to a thrilled Marky as he was to fuck Number One's impressive ass. In an instant, Marky was up Sen's fine forty-year-old awe-inspiring anus. Marky's eyes rolled back in his head.

"And I'm Number Three." Junior positioned himself behind Number Two. "Twenty-four ... and wanting more." Junior slammed his hips forward.

"Aaagh!"

Marky's face was a whirlwind of pain, pleasure, surprise, delight, amazement, and finally, total euphoria. "Oh, man, fucking and getting fucked. You guys have got to be the most totally awesome superheroes. What are you called? The Naked Duo?"

"That might work!" Junior exclaimed. He and Sen thought for a moment and then sighed, shaking their heads. "If only ..."

As hips swung back and forth and dicks shoved in and slid out, they explained.

"We're ladies in waiting," Junior smirked.

"We're fucking SuperHeroes in waiting," Senior snarled.

"We wait upon the pleasure of the League." Junior licked Marky's ear. "If a superhero ever retires, we'll get the chance to take his place ... maybe. There are real ladies waiting to take the girl superheroes' places."

"The only way to move ahead is to come up with a totally unique superhero," Sen noted glumly, rocking his ass back and forth so that his sphincter munched hungrily on Marky's very substantial prong, chewing it deeper. Marky groaned.

"Have you every tried that shit?" Junior demanded crossly, slamming even more forcefully forward, driving his super shaft deeper into Marky's ass. Marky yelped.

"After the corporate takeover, there was such a fucking proliferation of superheroes, it's impossible to come up with something that hasn't already been tried."

"We did everything we knew to do," Sen continued. "Got together in case there was a twosome that needed replacing. Bulked up. 'Course, cute ass here has still got his baby fat."

Annoyed, Junior pounded his prick into Marky, slamming the Number Two man forward.

"I feeeel your pain," Sen sang happily.

"They gave us some superhero powers to practice with while we're waiting, but they only last for a little while. Some sort of adrenaline thing the docs reprogrammed in us."

"You mean like the blowing and running through fire and the kissing so people forget?"

"Yeah," Sen murmured. "Say, Number Two, I've got this itch just a little deeper than ..."

"I can take care of that," Junior said. He bent his knees and using no hands lifted Marky off the floor with his dick, shoving Marky's meat so deep inside Sen's butt Sen could feel the extra thrust he had been looking for with the extra fillip of the deliveryman's substantial balls slapping against his butt cheeks. Marky gasped.

"Oh, yeah, that did it, partner." Sen smiled happily. "Thanks."

Huffing in oxygen and hanging onto the muscle-popping bookends for dear life, Marky choked out, "But what about the neighbors? You don't kiss them."

"Retired superheroes. Put out to pasture. Knowing they'll never be called up again. Golf and gardening. Great bunch of guys and gals. What a waste." Sen sighed. He could see the future, and it possibly didn't include his or Junior's ever having made the top grade.

There was tap on the high basement window. A craggy face peered in, saw the action and gave the trio thumbs up. Sen indicated for the visitor to come down as Junior waved.

The craggy face appeared around the doorway leading to the outside stairs.

"Sorry to interrupt, guys. Hey, you got a new recruit? Good luck, but don't hold your breath, son. Nice butt. Sen and Junior, Fluffy is at it again. She's got all the dogs howling with her squalls." He shrugged. "Whenever you get a chance, the folks around there would certainly appreciate the effort." His head pulled back, then reappeared. "Sen, your set of privates looks finer every time you display 'em. You want to stop by the house for a Senior Happy Hour one of these days...?"

"Floyd, you know that would negate our powers. But thanks for noticing. I think it's that new massage technique Junior uses. Maybe he could work on you? You're sure holding up nicely."

"The missus whips my ass every day to hit the plates. She can still out snatch me." He sighed, giving Sen's genitals one last look, Still..." Kissing his fingertips, he closed the door.

In answer to Marky's puzzled expression, Junior explained. "Floyd the Macho Hetero was assigned to superhero male sensitivity sessions when he showed signs of homophobia. Now he's retired and 'curious.' He doesn't know it, yet, but his missus isn't 'curious' with her girlfriends anymore. She knows."

"Jeez, this neighborhood sounds like a retired superheated soap opera."

"Hey, Desperate Superheroes." Sen pondered the TV possibilities. Then shook his head, knowing the League's reaction to the concept. "OK, boys, enough talk." He gripped the bar and spread his massive thighs wider. "Action, applicant. Hut, one; hut, two; hut, three."

Marky fucked the superass for all he was worth. Junior fucked the deliveryman's ass for all he was worth. They both fired off. Senior shot a load that sailed across the makeshift gym and splattered against a wall mirror ten feet away.

"You can imagine what that feels like down your throat or hosing up your butt," Sen smirked, pulling on a pair of snug workout shorts. "OK, let's go get the little girl's cat out of the tree."

* * * * *

Two years later, in the same basement work-out space, the weekly meeting of the neighborhood SuperDogs Night-No Girls Allowed (SuDONGa!) was just finishing up the final orgy of the evening as Sen and Junior moved among the energetic copulating couples and threesomes and foursomes of older and younger men, making suggestions regarding body positioning, stroke tempos, and depth of penetrations. They judged vocal reactions – leaning toward the more natural grunts and groans as opposed to the unoriginal cries of, "Yeah, man! Deeper, dude! and Harder, you shit head!" – and cautioned about overstraining various body organs and orifices.

The group consisted of the neighborhood old guys — having peeked into Sen and Junior's steamy basement action – who finally prevailed on the two men to share some of their super sex techniques with the swiftly diminishing abilities of the retirees. Junior recruited younger superdudes-to-be from various nearby areas, and soon a regular weekly gangbang was happening.

The orgasmic groans and gasps abated, and the sated members slowly rose one by one to stand as a body for the final communal buddy yell. "SuDONGa! SuDONGa! SuDONGa!" bounced off the walls as triumphal fists pumped the air and bumping, swinging hips swung drained dongs and emptied balls back and forth, followed by cheers and hoots for their instructors.

Senior and Junior took a bow.

The SuDONGa members began to dress and with affectionate hugs and back and butt slapping slowly filed out.

Floyd (now the Man's Man) stopped by to say goodnight. "That thing you showed me with the tongue. Drives the old lady crazy. Drove my partner tonight pretty crazy, too." He waved and winked at a cute, pug-nosed young stud waiting at the door. "You guys ever hear from that hunky DeliveryMan superhero buddy of yours?"

"Marky's doing great," Junior enthused. "I thought that was the dumbest idea ever, but the League said give it a try and turns out superfast delivering really important documents and medicines and supplies all over the universe was a fantastic concept."

"Frees the rest of the superhero pantheon from the grunt work," Sen added. "So everybody's grateful."

"Except you guys, right? Still waiting. Well, you sure saved the rest of our asses. A bunch of horny retirees not getting their rocks off and a bunch of young studs hanging around waiting to make use of their superpowers was not making for happy neighborhoods. Thanks, guys. My old lady thanks you, and my young studs thank you."

After a grateful hug, on his way out, Floyd picked up a group of eager young men who had gathered waiting for him. They all yelled goodnight.

At the head of the basement stairs, Junior switched off the lights. "You think this is what we are supposed to be doing? Saving a bunch of guys' sex lives?"

With a chuckle, Sen grabbed the young man and threw him over his shoulder, feeling the punch of his buddy's powerful protrusion. Affectionately, he patted the powerful young rump. "I feeeel your protrusion. And we are saving and supercharging, superstud. Hey, what do you think the corporate suits would say to that suggestion? SuperSexHeroes! All over world, speeding to where bad timing and rotten aim cause pain. Perfecting techniques. Promoting sexual health among the races and classes and sexes. Bringing the whole universe together in one gigantic orgy."

Junior whooped, before doffing his shorts and hopping off Sen's shoulder to reach down and strip his senior buddy. He easily picked up the naked older man and tossed him into bed.

"Naagh. If everybody was having a great time fucking and sucking, they wouldn't have time to be bad guys. What would happen to the rest of the superheroes? They'd never wear out, and we'd never get in. Let's just keep it in the neighborhood."

His rosy lips stretched wide and slipped over his older buddy's meat.

All the way down.

Super deep throated, Sen leaned back, super thighs wide, super biceps bulging on arms folded contentedly behind his head.

"Hmm, maybe you're right."

But he wondered ...

M/M Mathmen!
By Troy Storm

"But I want to wear tights. All superdudes wear tights."

My pouting buddy was superbright about math – super genius bright – but even though this hero stuff was new to the both of us, I knew he couldn't wear tights.

"Pauly, your dick is too big. And your balls. You'd look like you packed a way too hot lunch. That might not exactly inspire confidence in the nuclear command center guys."

He smirked. "What if we get there at lunchtime? They might be feeling a little ... hungry." I was not amused. Pauly glared at me and turned back to the full-length mirror on our bedroom closet door.

"I look like a dad-gummed nerd in this stupid suit and tie. And you can still tell I've got a big dick." He shook his left leg. You sure could.

I swallowed. "Well, don't shake your leg, then, doofus." Pauley's dick was becoming a thing between us. Didn't I wish.

Pauley and I were math geniuses, but most of the time, he acted like he didn't even know he had a dick, much less obsess about it the way I was doing now.

We were both dedicated and serious about our work, but even with the relaxed standards the Council allowed for same-sex researchers, we had never made a pass at each other, though I have to admit, I had looked. Pauley was not bad looking. In fact, Pauley was hot.

But I had not seen – the dick.

And now I had to get my mind off what had suddenly been revealed to me and had produced the same body-rattling electric shock as the mind-boggling thrill of discovering a new formula – Pauley's fantastic physique and his huge manpole and wonder balls.

It was hard to take it all in – so to speak – since there was so much of his equipment to suddenly think about, to imagine all the things that could be done with and to.

If only ...

But I had to concentrate on more important matters, on our mission, on the special assignment with which we and we alone had been entrusted: to save the world.

Well, maybe not exactly the whole world – but a very big part.

For just a moment, I forgot about Pauley's third leg and had a flush of importance. We ... us ... the nerd team of the age had been frantically gotten in touch with by the Council to do something exciting and practical – for a fucking change.

I loved working with my numbers and symbols and – to everyone else but Pauley, my closest buddy and co-researcher – my incomprehensible formulas. But we were the only ones on this particular planet who could possible avert the impending doom, and we had been called ... albeit, a little ... dramatically.

"You wouldn't have ever known I had a big dick – and balls – if that explosion in the math lab hadn't burned off all our clothes. You never paid that much attention to me, anyway," he grumbled.

I tightened my dumb tie against my bobbing Adam's Apple and reached inside my jacket to straighten the pocket protector, bulging with pens and pencils at the ready.

"Pauley, I noticed you. I notice you now. You're a great guy, you were a fantastic guy even before we became superheroes, but ... well, it's hard for me to concentrate on two things at once, and before we were busy researching, and now we've got this important job to do."

"You've got a big dick, too, you know," he muttered. "And big balls, too." He followed me out of the bedroom. "Maybe even bigger than mine. And I knew that even before that blast turned us into superheroes and got you naked."

"How did you know?"

"Well ... sometimes you leave the door to the bathroom open when you're showering, so you won't steam up the mirror."

"And you peeked. Whoa. Did you ever catch me jacking off?"

"Yeah. But you were turned away. You've got a great ass, too."

Pauley had a fantastic ass. In those cheap, threadbare tighty-whities he wore, you could tell those muscular butt melons of his were hard and solid and hairy and ... but I sure never thought he had noticed mine before. Damn.

We hurried down the basement stairs into the demolished math lab. I cringed at the mess. The Council hadn't really known what they were doing when they beamed us the alarm signal. We were pretty far down the list of specialists to be called in an emergency, which I guess was why their signals weren't up to date, and they blew the bejesus out of our equipment.

Oh, well, it made us superheroes – at least for the time being – and we got a couple of really hot outfits to wear – or at least I did. If we pulled this emergency off, we might be awarded more powers – and we might figure out how to calm down Pauley's dick, so he could play dress-up, too.

"Big dick and big nuts," Pauley continued to grumble as we grabbed mini-chutes and strapped ourselves into Ducky Lucky, one of the few pieces of equipment that hadn't been totally wrecked. "I don't see why you get to wear tights if I don't."

"Because my dick isn't half-hard all the time like yours is, Pauley. And we may have to resort to that superhero stuff to make the power plant guys pay attention to us. Is your mind always on sex, now?"

He snickered. "Only since the explosion last night. That blast really grabbed my gonads. Didn't it yours? Man, I am horny and ready to go anytime. Isn't that a hoot?"

Hoot? Hell, I was super horny, too, but I couldn't tell him. What good would it do? We had a mission to accomplish, and taking care of each other's "hoots" was not part of the job description. Not now.

With a rattle and shake of its battered frame, the ever-trustworthy trans-M transport unit – Ducky Lucky – cranked up, the digital touch screen counted us down, and we shot into a low orbit, locking onto the magnetic bands of migration patterns.

Pauley punched some figures into his fanny pack (another nerd piece of our personal equipment), and we sailed over oceans and scattered islands and headed for the foreign mainland.

The indicator lamps attached to our narrow lapels began to sputter – we were being jammed as expected – and began to lose altitude, but we had made it across and were over our target. Tightening the straps that passed over our chests and through our crotches, we activated our mini-chutes. I checked our final destination coordinates, punched them into the locator in my fanny pack, and we gently floated down toward the countryside.

A hunky, bare-chested farmhand came running up to meet us. Boy, the Council really knew how to pick its operatives. He had been alerted to our arrival. Spouting his native tongue, eyes narrowed, he paid no attention to me and jumped up to grab Pauley, locking his grip onto my buddy's bulging elongated package outlined halfway down his left leg.

A gasp. A blush. A torrent of apologies. A chuckle on Pauley's part, and we all landed in a heap. I slipped the wireless translator into my ear, but my horny buddy was busy smiling and nodding and trying to communicate in our own pidgin language.

"He thought that was where you might be carrying a weapon," I told Pauley flatly, explaining to the bare-chested dude we had no weapons, but did need directions. The stud shrugged and poked at Pauley's meat. Was it really all real? He had heard superheroes were hung like stallions, but well, I didn't look quite as well-endowed. Was I truly a member of the mission and was Pauley truly that well equipped?

Pauley looked smugly over at me, then happily pulled his massive manhood out to show the stud, who instantly fell to his knees in total worship. I had to admit, sticking out of Pauley's nerd suit, his dick looked every inch the gut-choker it turned out to be. The guy asked nicely, if frantically time was of the essence – but sex, of course, was even more essence-er. Pauley pulled out his balls, too (superballs now), and let the guy have at his super equipment. It was important to keep on good terms with the operatives we dealt with, he gasped – unnecessarily, I thought – as this particular hot operative sucked in half his meat and proceeded to vacuum the seed right out of Pauley's nuts.

There was nothing to do but watch. I pulled out my pitifully ordinary (compared to Pauley's) prick, stroked it a couple of times to make sure it was functional, then pounded the hell out of it until I had hosed a load onto the muscular operative's naked back.

He didn't even notice. He was busy taking a gutful from Pauley, whose drop-jawed, half-lidded response to blowing a load reminded me of Daumier drawings of bedlam inmates. Crazy fucker. I, myself, held myself in check a bit better when I spewed my seed, I smugly noted to myself.

The grinning dude wiped Pauley's cum from his chin and started giving us our instructions while pulling IDs for us out of his pants. I wouldn't have minded checking out what was inside the dude's loose-fits, but now that Pauley's dick had gone down pretty much to a normal porn dog size, he was all business and ready to move on.

A few kilometers later, we hopped off the scooter that had been pulled out of hiding and snuck around the perimeter of the target complex. Most of the reactors in that region had little security because what difference would it make, considering all the methods of destruction that had been devised by then? So it was fairly easy showing our fake IDs to the not-very-interested local security and getting inside.

The six men at the controls were another matter. They explained, courteously, but definitively, we weren't going to be allowed near the panels. In desperation, Pauley explained how the World International Terrorists League of Extreme Supreme Solutions (WITLESS) had been able to crack the security code and wirelessly remotely reconfigure the controls of the string of reactors. On their secret signals, the complex would be shut down, causing meltdown and thus depriving most of the region of electricity. Indefinitely. Chaos would ensue.

The controllers didn't believe us, but after some spirited conferring among themselves in their native tongue – and asking us politely to step to the other side of the room – they began to run a series of highly classified diagnostics. Shockingly, our pronouncement proved true.

However, Pauley and I weren't yet home free. It was time to show our credentials. I stripped off my suit and blazed forth in the M/M MATHMEN spandex. We were newly created SuperHero math geniuses who had been called from our lonely lab by the InterGallactic Supreme Council (IGCS) to fly forth and prevent this terrible catastrophe.

Pauley beamed at my powerful stance and my ringing pronouncement. His left leg began to shake.

Wow. Seeing me in my spandex had given my buddy a big hard bone. Kewl.

Wow. Watching his meat swell, it was all I could do to hold in my own stiffening sausage.

But the band of controller dudes was too distracted by something else to notice Pauley's predicament and mine. They were howling with laughter at the logo scrawled across my chest.

M/M to them meant "Men on Men." As in M/M/W for man, man, woman (threeway), they explained, or perhaps M/W/M/W (fourway), a couple of leering ones further explained, or yet M/M/M/M/M/M (sixway). A handsome, hunky dude squeezed the broad shoulders of his nearby co-workers and kissed them soundly on their blushing cheeks before sliding his hands down their backs to smack them affectionately on their butts.

All the men chuckled and shrugged. It got lonely at the plant, with them stuck in the control room by themselves, just guys – six months on, six months off. Obviously, they would need an outlet for their sexual proclivities. Their bosses didn't mind what outlet they chose, so sometimes – often – pretty much daily – they got less lonely – wink, wink – if we knew what they meant.

What did the M/M mean to us? They demanded. Uh, well, why, superhero Math/Men, of course, we explained – glancing at each other but obviously keeping in mind their explanation.

As further proof, Pauley and I threw back and forth some abstruse mathematical nuclear formulae, which indeed did seem to impress the expert controllers with our expertise.

OK, but why was I the only one wearing a superhero outfit? One that emphasized my full-blown sexual equipment. Was I the dominating one? How did I dominate him? Were we also, as they were, sex buddies? Did we, you know, do it like superheroes? How did superheroes do it?

Pauley and I put our heads together. It was obviously time to reveal our super masculine sexuality as well as our mathematical genius.

He pulled out his monster masher, explaining that the Council had not known it was too impressive to be held in check by the spandex, but that I, in my patriotic fervor was doing what I could to keep it under control for the mission.

Pauley and I would therefore demonstrate how I manfully took it up the butt. He doused the throbbing, vein-choked, meaty column with half a tube of lube. The purple nosecone was already dripping. I slipped my superhero costume from my shoulders and peeled it down to bare my tense ass cheeks and bent over, presenting myself for his impalement. The other half of the tube of lube went onto the fingers of both of my impaler's hands, which dug into my hole to ream me wide.

We had no idea whether the butt fuck was going to work or not – needless to say, we had not previously indulged – but the men were glued to our demonstration. Pauley aimed. I pulled 'em apart, my sphincter split wide, and he punctured my ass.

I took it like a superhero.

The men cheered, impressed with the tears pouring down my cheeks and the ass juices squeezed out and pouring down my nether cheeks. They surrounded us, slapping Pauley on the back, giving me kisses on both sets of wet cheeks while leaning in to observe closely and compare notes on the awesome super dick that slowly pumped in and out of the super sucking butt hole.

With the group satisfied with our credentials, Pauley extracted his honker. Damn. I was hoping my ass would be so enticing he would at least give me a quickie.

We hooked up our minicomputers to the control boards and rewrote the circuits for the entire chain of reactors. The bad guys wouldn't even know. Hopefully, they would expose themselves in expecting a meltdown, and when it didn't come would be an easy catch for the locals.

After we had accomplished our mission, we announced we should quickly return to our home base to notify the Council since communication was blocked here. The men – bless each and every enthusiastic, sexy one of them – would have none of it.

They broke out the happy brew, and for the next couple of hours Pauley and I fucked and got fucked by the "super six" until everybody was pretty much super screwed. We left with many manly hugs and exchanges of emails.

"You didn't fuck me once," I groused, while we were waiting in the field for our return flight on Ducky Lucky that evening.

"Well, gee, you didn't fuck me, either. But you sure took care of that muscle dude with the hairy butt. How many – three, four times? He wouldn't let me get near him."

"You were pretty awesome," I smiled. "You know, Pauley, the more action you get, the more your giant dick returns to normal. Maybe that means you might be able to wear the spandex after all."

He thought about it – us constantly sexing it up to keep his dick down. "Gee, you think? Oh, man, how can I thank you?"

"I could suck you off while we're waiting," I replied slyly. "Maybe that would help cut down on our wind resistance on the way back."

"Kewl." Pauley's thick lashes fluttered, and his thick dick flapped forth. I got down on my hands and knees, opened my drooling lips, and in he went.

The huge head filled my mouth, ironing my tongue down as it snuggled into my throat. The throbbing veins pressed against the inside of my cheeks as I valiantly sucked.

Pauley whimpered.

"Oh, man, that is so good."

I opened my throat. He slid in further. Then I pulled my mouth back up the length of hard meat, my lips tight against the stretched flesh, leaving just the greasy tip inside, thrashing it with my tongue and digging into the cavernous piss-slit.

Pauley growled. I sucked him in again, this time ingesting even more of his amazing fuckpole. I began to pump my head, with each forward stroke guzzling even more meaty inches.

Suddenly, I realized I was going to eat the whole damn thing!

Pauley was trembling he was so thrilled.

My nose drove into his wiry mat of pubic hair. The head of his dick seemed tucked inside my chest. I chewed the root like mad.

The beam of a harsh flashlight hit us. "What is going on?" a thick accent enquired. We froze.

Two local policemen strolled around us. With my face completely encompassing Pauley's gut-gouging equipment they couldn't really tell what was going on, other than I had my head in his crotch. I started flapping my arms and fiddling with his fanny pace.

"He's, uh, trying to adjust the transducer of the transmigratory transponder." Pauley began spouting scientific sounding garbage as I nodded intently and kept my face jammed against him. The dick inside my mouth and throat and down my gut was getting bigger and bigger from excitement. Soon all oxygen would be cut off, and I would be dead meat dangling on a dynamite dong. What a way to go!

The local cop nodded knowingly at his gobbledygook jargon as Pauley kept up the patter explaining how we were visiting nuclear inspectors and were waiting for our return transport.

"In the middle of an empty field in the middle of the night?" the less gullible policemen asked sternly.

At that moment, Ducky Lucky floated down out of the night sky on its own set of mini-chutes. Pauley yanked his dick out of my throat as oxygen flooded deep into my grateful lungs, grabbed me, and we leapt onto the transport platform.

The cops charged us, shouting stop. As we quickly ascended into the darkness, Pauley let loose a volley of cum shots that arced snow white against the velvet black of the night sky to splatter over the attacking officers. Realizing they were being cummed, they ducked and ran, howling obscenities.

The super heroes sailed away, mission completed.

* * * * *

"How do I look?" Pauley smiled proudly into our bedroom mirror, as only a splendidly spandexed superhero who – along with his partner in preventive crime – was to be presented to the Council for a Special Commendation medal, could beam.

"You're still pretty big down there, Mighty Mathman. I might have to suck you off again."

Pauley grinned slyly and began to peel down his glittering super garb. "You've sucked me off three times already this morning. Why don't we give your jaws a rest, and I fuck you in the ass?"

Holy Anal Entry, I had completely forgotten about my butt on this magic morning. I had been totally obsessed with having accomplished the super feat of being able to swallow my buddy's sword in its entirety – and breathe at the same time.

He squirted in the lube as I aimed my butt hole. The protective muscular cheeks spread wide, and the glory hole automatically opened.

We were both anything but prime nerd examples, now. Having taken full assessment of our superbods, we worked the weights with the same concentration we applied to our foiling destructive math situations worldwide.

We were both muscle-popping hot.

Pauley smoothed the glittering M/M MATHMEN! logo over his newly-chiseled pecs and ran his fingers through the dark, glossy waves of his also-new, more free-flowing haircut than the close-clipped, practical nerd dos we had worn before.

"Satisfied with yourself, stud?" I snuggled against his front, plucking at the prominent tented nipples pressing their tasty nubs hard against the thick super fabric.

"Now we look like we belong." He beamed. "I wouldn't mind appearing at any mall to sign autographs, now."

I playfully punched him in his tight six-pack and then let my hand skim down to cup his crotch. The thick shaft of his rising dick nestled against my palm. His shapely dick-head rose to press against my middle fingers, dividing the twin ovals of his outstanding nuts that nudged hard against my thumb and little finger. In a few minutes, he was going to be unacceptable in public again.

"You want to go for one last flying fuck before the big event?" He cradled my butt in his hands and pulled me close. We had less than an hour. Time enough. I nodded and sucked his tit through the clinging stretch fabric while digging my hand more firmly into his hot lunch.

That was a yes since our "flying fuck" was special. Other super heroes might do it their own way – enough of them could fly – but, even though we didn't have that ability, we had a specially rigged Ducky Lucky and a choice of migratory patterns that made slamming our beef among the clouds our own unique event.

Watching himself in the bedroom mirror, Pauley peeled his M/M MATHMEN! outfit down to his thighs. I barely got mine down past my butthole before he had flipped me around and plugged me from the rear. Clumsily, but butt happily, I fumbled my superhero outfit off my legs and tied it around my waist while Pauley pistoned in and out. He grabbed my nipples and hung on as I leaned forward, swinging my arms up before me. I kicked up my legs and locked my ankles behind his butt, stretching out my body. My ass cheeks tightened around Pauley's buried bone like a lock wrench securing a twelve-inch bolt.

He worked his outfit the rest of the way off his legs – while not losing a stroke of fucking my butt – and reached down to secure the shrunken elastic fabric around one of his now massive thighs. With a happy howl, he took off out of the bedroom – me swimming in the air in front of him – galloping down the stairs to our refurbished basement math lab.

"Hi ya, Ducky Lucky," he saluted the shining contraption, "we're starting the celebration early with one last civilian ducky fucky." Leaping onto the platform with me still skewered on his rock-hard projectile, he secured his feet into the special brackets we had installed. I rested my chest on the padded incline board and spread my legs wide in a swan dive position as Pauley slipped his wrists through the handholds and kicked Ducky into gear.

We took off, a naked, fucking double masthead sailing high, honing in on a migratory pattern that would take us into the atmosphere then loop us back in plenty of time for the ceremony.

Pauley howled like a banshee, driving in and out of me with a super power that rammed my pole out like a guided missile. He grabbed my dick and pounded the steaming flesh in rhythm with his fucking. Ducky found a flock of cruising geese, and we sailed in and out of the squawking birds spraying them with fountains of cum as Pauley got me off, time and time again, while he creamed my clutching colon with his super seed.

Who says guys can't have multiple organisms?

Who says nerds can't become super heroes?

Right on ... into the blue ... M/M MATHMEN!

Jackal vs. Thresher: The Reckoning
By Christopher Pierce

Jackal didn't know if the pounding in his ears was blood in his veins or the storm outside. Rain pelted the roof of the abandoned warehouse, creating sounds of hundreds of feet sprinting across the surface.

Although outside it had been chilly, inside the warehouse, Jackal could feel sweat drip from his forehead and crawl down his bare arms. He felt its moisture all over his body, from his hairy chest to the pouch under his clothes that held his cock and balls. The feeling would almost be sensual if he hadn't been aware he might die in the next few minutes.

Jackal took a deep breath and gazed at the man standing across from him. About fifteen feet of floor separated them as they stood facing each other motionless.

Thresher stood there, watching him.

Just like every time they met, Jackal couldn't help feeling attracted to Thresher. He was tall, over six feet, with silvery gray skin that shimmered whenever light touched it. His face was handsome, and his body heavily muscled. Between his legs, his dick and nuts hung proudly, stuffed into a too-tight jockstrap that was the same color as the rest of his body. The gill-slits on his neck flexed rhythmically as they drew in air.

But his eyes – Jackal tried not to look at Thresher's hypnotic eyes – so light blue they were almost white. Cold they were, burning with an icy fire. Even this far away, Jackal felt as if he could see himself reflected in those eyes, see himself as Thresher saw him – shorter, 5'8" or so, stocky and muscular, most of his body covered with a thick pelt of bristly fur; his eyes, hair and fur all the same shade of dark brown. A tattered black tank top and black jockstrap were his only coverings besides the heavy boots on his feet.

Superhero and Supervillain faced each other, both taking deep breaths before what could be their last battle.

"This's been a long time coming," Jackal said to break the silence.

"Yes," Thresher said, "I'm going to make you pay for what you did."

"You know I had no choice."

"Save your words, animal. Your time has come."

Thresher launched himself at Jackal, who tried to dart out of the way. But he wasn't fast enough, and Thresher's arm grazed his own. Like the shark whose name he shared, the Supervillain's sharp skin was rough enough to tear flesh.

Jackal grunted in pain and whirled to face his opponent. He flexed his hand muscles and two-foot claws sprang from his fingertips. Snarling, he brandished his claws and charged. Thresher was ready for him and blocked his slash with one muscular arm.

Thresher seized his opponent and crushed him to his chest. Jackal struggled and screamed as Thresher's skin tore into his own. The gray man ground his jockstrap-covered groin in the furry man's, and Jackal's cock responded against his will. The friction of their two dicks, even covered in fabric, was powerful enough for the two men to moan with desire. Jackal snarled at the man holding him and spat his next words at him.

"Let me go! I won't let you complete your evil plan!"

Thresher squeezed him harder and growled.

"Don't fight me! This is what you want, don't deny yourself. Look at me!"

Jackal furiously looked away, the wall, the ceiling, anything but those eyes …

"Look into my eyes, animal, or I'll shred you to pieces right here and now!"

Helplessly, the furry man looked up into the gray man's eyes. The irises blazed with blue fire, and Jackal suddenly felt a change in his enemy's body. The harsh rough surface of Thresher's skin was becoming smooth, like that of a dolphin rather than a shark. The sensation was strange and exhilarating.

"I ... I didn't know you could do that ..." he gasped.

"I'm full of surprises," Thresher said as he leaned down to kiss the other man. Jackal wanted to resist, tried to resist, but it was impossible – his opponent's eyes burning into him, his strong arms wrapped around him, the suddenly smooth body against his, and their throbbing cocks grinding together through the fabric of their jockstraps.

The Supervillain pushed his tongue into the Superhero's mouth and probed inside. Jackal welcomed the invasion and returned his enemy's embrace.

This can't be happening, he thought, *I shouldn't be doing this!* But, he was helpless against Thresher's powerful sexuality, and he kissed him back, hard. The taller man growled in triumph as his affection was returned.

Thresher put his hands on his enemy's shoulders and pushed him down to the floor. Jackal sank to his knees obediently until his face was level with the taller man's crotch. He looked at the bulging jockstrap, and unable to resist, pulled it out and down. Thresher's hands stayed on Jackal's shoulders, although the furry man made no attempt to escape. When his rival's magnificent cock was released from its fabric prison, Jackal stared at it for a moment, enthralled as always by its power and beauty.

"Suck it, animal," Thresher growled above him, "You know you want to."

The furry man opened his mouth and took the huge organ inside himself. Jackal made love to his enemy's dick, slurping and sucking on it until its owner was rumbling with pleasure. Thresher put his hands on Jackal's head and started face-fucking him, thrusting his cock deep into the smaller man's mouth. The Superhero made no noise of protest as he was savagely used.

Grabbing the sides of the furry man's head, the Supervillain forced his dick all the way into Jackal's mouth and shot a huge load down his throat. He roared in triumph, as his orgasm shuddered through his powerful body. Jackal held Thresher's cock in his mouth until the gray man's shudders subsided. Gently, he let the tremendous organ slide out of his mouth and prepared to stand up.

"I hope this means you want to discuss a truce ..." Jackal started as he stood up. But Thresher threw something over his enemy's head that enclosed him completely.

"Think again, animal," the Supervillain said as he brought the bag all the way down around Jackal's body, "I told you I'm full of surprises."

"Oh damn," Jackal said as he felt his powers ebbing away. He knew he'd been trapped in a stunsack, one of Thresher's nefarious inventions. Any Superhero that was caught inside a stunsack was rendered immobile and temporarily drained of his powers. Jackal cursed himself as he felt his enemy secure the bag around his feet. *Caught so easily!* He thought. *When am I going to learn?*

The furry man, fully stuffed into the bag, felt his enemy pick up the stunsack and sling it over his shoulder. His mission accomplished, Thresher carried the bag containing his rival out of the warehouse into the storm where his vehicle was waiting.

* * * * *

Jackal awoke to find himself strapped to a table with a light glaring into his eyes. He struggled against his bonds but found that not only were his arms and legs restricted, but also his neck was held down by a metal collar-like device. The Superhero couldn't even turn or raise his head.

"Thresher!" he yelled.

His adversary's voice came from close by, but he couldn't see him.

"Why can't you call me by my real name?" he asked.

"Thresher is your real name."

"No more than your real name is Jackal, it isn't," Thresher said.

"I don't know what you're talking about."

Threshed laughed without humor.

"Do I have to remind you what happened on the night of February 3, 2005?"

No, he didn't.

How could Jackal forget the night everything changed?

It had been two years ago, up at the lake where he'd inherited the summer cabin his parents had taken him to when he was a kid. He and Justin, his boyfriend of five years, had been skinny-dipping in the lake.

The two young men swam out past the dock to where the water was deeper. Justin looked up at the night sky with wonder.

"Look at all those stars, man," he said, "I can't believe how bright they are."

"It's beautiful, huh?"

"When you live in the city all your life, you forget to look at the sky."

They stopped and treaded water for a few minutes in silence. Then Justin took the other young man in his arms.

"I love you, Thomas," he said.

"I love you, too."

"On nights like these ... it feels like almost anything can happen."

They had leaned in to kiss each other when a light as bright as the sun suddenly flared from the sky, and a sound like thunder roared down with it.

"What the hell?" Justin yelled above the noise.

Thomas was pointing at the sky.

"Justin, look! It's a meteor!"

"It's gonna hit the lake!" Justin yelled, "We've got to get out of here!"

"God, look how beautiful it is ..."

"Thomas, come on! That son-of-a-bitch is as big as a house, and it's heading straight for us!"

Justin had to grab his lover and drag him back through the water toward the dock. Thomas was mesmerized by the meteor, his eyes glazed as its fiery light covered the whole lake.

"It's here ..." Thomas said, as if in prayer.

The meteor slammed into the lake and displaced water shot hundreds of feet into the air around it. The noise was deafening as giant waves were forced outward from the point of impact.

"Oh shit," Justin said as he wrapped his arms around his lover's torso. "We're not gonna make it, Thomas, hold on to me!"

The wave caught the two men and swept them up in its roiling embrace. Somehow Justin kept his grip on Thomas as the water slammed and crashed around them. They were hurled forward by the force of the wave and soon found themselves on the lake's shore, gasping for breath.

"My God ... I've never ..." Justin said, "Thomas, what are you doing?"

Thomas had gotten to his feet, and was staring at his arms and body like he'd never seen them before.

"What is it?" Justin asked.

"I don't know," Thomas said, "I feel different."

Justin stopped for a minute and then said "Hey, me, too."

"What's happened?"

"I have no idea," Justin said, "but I feel stronger somehow, stronger than I've ever felt."

Thomas pointed out onto the lake, where the water was still boiling angrily, and the meteor's glow was still visible despite the chunk of rock's having sunk to the bottom.

"Justin," he asked, "could the meteor have ... changed us ... somehow?"

"Fuck if I know," Justin said, "but I feel like I have new muscles, ones I've never flexed before."

"Me, too," Thomas said, "but maybe we shouldn't …"

"Why not?" Justin said, "Let's see what happens."

"No …"

Before Thomas's eyes, his lover changed. Justin's skin changed into the razor-sharp hide of a shark. His body bulged with muscles and gill-slits appeared on his neck. Thomas stared as his lover's cock lengthened from its already sizable girth to a monstrous and mouth-watering size. Justin's eyes blazed with blue fire, and his whole body dulled in color to a silvery gray, again like a shark's body.

"Do it, Thomas," he said, "Flex your new muscles. See what you've been gifted with."

"I …"

"Do it!"

Thomas obeyed and willed his new powers to exert themselves. He found strength flowing into his muscles like he'd never felt before. Fur sprang from his body as if he were a werewolf, the hairy pelt covering nearly every inch of him. He flexed harder and found his ears growing longer and pointing up, like those of a wild dog … or a jackal. Deadly razor-sharp claws sprang from his fingers, powerful weapons that could kill with one strike. He felt more alive than he ever had in his life, and gazed at his lover, breathing hard.

"Look at you," Justin said, "You're beautiful."

"How could this have happened?" Thomas asked.

"I don't know," Justin said, "But I do know one thing."

"What's that?"

"That right now I want to fuck you more than I've ever wanted anything in my life …"

Thomas' voice was full of doubt. "But shouldn't we …"

Justin stepped up to him and put his hand over the other man's mouth.

"Should?" he said, laughing. "There's no more should. And if there is, we'll decide it."

"What are you talking about?"

"Don't you understand?" Justin said. "Everything's different now. We've got strength, powers, beyond anything the world's ever seen. We can rule this world, you and me, Thomas!"

"No, it's wrong, Justin, we can't use our powers to hurt people. If anything, we should help them!"

"I don't believe what I'm hearing!" Justin said, advancing on his lover threateningly. "What about all those nights we played Supervillain, plotting to take over the world?"

"Those were just games, Justin! This is reality, we can't ..."

"Can't!?" Justin roared. "I never want to hear that word again, Thomas! There's nothing I can't do!"

Justin threw his lover down onto the ground and pounced on him. He shoved his cock into the other man. Thomas screamed in pain as his lover fucked him harder than he ever had before. Justin's sharp skin cut him, and he bled. They both climaxed, Justin shooting his seed into Thomas, and Thomas shooting his onto the blood-stained ground.

When it was over, Justin stood up and pulled his lover up as well. They looked at the water, which was still glowing with the sunken meteor's radiance.

"This is our new beginning," Justin said.

"Is it?" Thomas asked.

"Now, we can finally strike back at all those who hurt us."

Thomas stepped away from Justin.

"What do you mean, we?" he asked.

* * * * *

"OK, Justin," Jackal said from the table he was tied to. "What do you want?"

"I want you."

Jackal checked that his neck, wrists and ankles were still bound to the table. "You appear to have me. Now what are you going to do with me?"

Thresher walked into his enemy's line of sight and looked down at him. Thomas saw that he had reverted to regular human form, just as the stunsack had done the same to him.

"I'm going to talk some sense into you," he said.

"I'm never going to be a Supervillain with you, Thresher," Jackal said, and Justin flinched at the name.

"I love you, goddamn you!" Justin yelled.

"And this is how you show it?" Thomas asked incredulously. "You trick me into sucking you off, stuff me in a bag, carry me back to your lair, and tie me to a table? What kind of love is that?"

"It's the only kind you respond to," Justin said defiantly, but Thomas could hear the doubt in his voice.

"Before we changed, you were gentle and caring with me ..." Thomas said. "The meteor changed more than your body and your abilities, Justin ... it changed your nature. You're not the same man I fell in love with."

Thresher roared with anger and hit the switch on a control panel near the table. Electricity flashed through the manacles on the table, and Jackal howled with pain.

"The man I fell in love with would never do this to me!" he screamed. Thresher hit the control, and the electricity died. He slumped next to the table, his head bowed in shame and despair.

"You may be the one tied up," he said, "but I'm the prisoner."

"Justin," Jackal panted through the lingering pain, "you know me. I'll never join you in your evil plans. I won't become a Supervillain."

"I love you ..." Thresher whispered.

"And I love you," Jackal said, "but I won't turn evil. I don't know why the meteor chose us. I don't know if there was any sense in what happened that night, but I've made my choice. I have and will continue to use my powers for good. To protect the weak, to defend the defenseless and to fight evil wherever it lurks, even in the man I love."

Thresher touched another control on his panel and Jackal felt the manacles release him from the table. He stood up and looked down at Thresher with love and regret.

"I know what drives you, Justin," he said. When Thresher looked up, there were tears in his eyes.

"You do?"

"Yes. Will you trust me?"

Justin nodded, and was amazed when his former lover picked him up, cradling him in his arms. Despite his smaller size, Thomas was incredibly strong and carried him easily. Thomas carried Justin to the bed that was tucked into a corner of the lair and lay him down. Then he got onto the bed and wrapped his arms around the larger man.

"I know why you chose to use your powers for evil, Justin." Thomas said.

"You do?"

"You want to pay back all the people who ever hurt you. Every person who ever called you faggot, every bully that beat you up after school, every lawmaker who ignored you and your needs, every powerbroker who denied you your rights, every holy man who said you were an abomination."

"Us!" Justin said, "I did it for us, for all gay people!"

"But did they ask you to?" Thomas said. "Hate, fear and violence only breed more of themselves. There are better ways to make ourselves known."

Thresher started crying.

"You don't have to be the avenger of all gay people, Justin," Thomas whispered. "It's OK to just be who you are."

"You said you still loved me …" Justin said.

"Yes," Thomas said, "and I always will."

They kissed, and Thomas gently lifted Justin's legs up, so he could slide between them. He removed the Supervillain's jockstrap and put his nose and mouth against his enemy's asshole. He made love to it, licking it and nuzzling it until it was open and ready.

Thomas pushed himself inside Justin and fucked him, gently – the opposite of the way he'd been fucked on the night of the meteor.

"It doesn't always have to be about power," he whispered. "Sometimes, it can be about tenderness."

He took Justin's huge cock in his hand and fisted it, feeling its power and majesty grow in his hand. The inside of Justin's body was cold like ice, but it was hot ice – Thomas's cock felt as if it were on fire inside of him.

Justin thrashed his head around as he was brought closer and closer to orgasm, but Thomas pulled back each time, not letting him finish no matter how much he begged.

"You're mine, Justin," Thomas said, "as much as I'm yours."

Then he forced himself into the other man as far as he could go, and wrapped him in his arms, crushing their chests together.

"Cum for me, evil one," Thomas whispered, and the roar that Justin made shook the foundations off the building. Superjizz spurted out of his cock, soaking the bed, the walls, the ceiling and his lover alike. Thomas held Justin as he came, feeling his own ejaculation rocket through him as he emptied his Superspunk into his enemy.

When they were done and Thomas had pulled out, he noticed that Justin's cock was getting hard again.

"Thirsty for more?" Thomas asked, and saw a familiar fire in his rival's eyes.

"I'm going to fuck your brains out, protector of the weak," Justin said, and he pounced on Thomas. He forced him on his stomach and plunged his dick deep inside his enemy. Justin reached under and grabbed Thomas' cock, jerking it hard.

"C'mon, animal," he growled. "You know you love this!"

And he did.

The Superhero and the Supervillain made love all night, climaxing many times, until they lay spent and exhausted in each other's arms.

"What happened?" Thresher asked in the morning.

"You remembered to look at the sky," Jackal said.

"What?"

"I showed you there are other ways to be. There's a whole world of possibilities out there, Justin. Our paths are not set. We can choose what we do."

Thresher stood up.

"This isn't over," he said.

"I know."

"One night of hot sex with my arch enemy isn't going to change me instantly," Thresher said.

"I know. But maybe it planted a seed in your mind, a seed that might grow."

Thresher flexed his powers, and his skin sharpened into shark-hide. His eyes blazed with blue fire.

Jackal got up off the bed, fur growing from his body and claws sprouting from his fingers.

Thresher raised his hand in salute, and Jackal did the same.

"Until we meet again," Thresher said.

"'Til then," Jackal agreed.

Master Mind

By Jay Starre

Master Mind lived a life of controlled chaos. As a private detective, he often dealt with the dregs of society. He was not all that sympathetic with the perverts and the losers he came into contact with.

"Get a life. Get it together. Stop whining and start taking some responsibility for your actions. Stop blaming everyone else for your problems."

He didn't say that out loud, of course. But it was often an effort not to broadcast those harsh thoughts into the minds of criminals and conmen he confronted regularly.

As for his need for control, it was a simple matter for him to bombard an unwilling victim with his powerful thoughts – his broadcasts as he labeled them. That was not always wise – or kind.

And worse, for him at least, he could pluck out thoughts from unwilling victims almost effortlessly. This also was never wise, or kind, and required more control.

Stormy afternoons were the worst. He was in Kansas, which was not the best place to be in the spring when storms threatened. The air was electric, the clouds heavy to the south with their burden of rain, and even though it was midday, it suddenly looked as if it was close to dark.

The farmhouse dominating the rolling fields below was no barn. It was a fucking mansion, Master Mind thought to himself. He smiled as he parked his car and surveyed the elaborate entrance. The man he investigated owned this ostentatious palace in the midst of rural obscurity. It seemed a little too obvious that the dude must be guilty as accused.

A gust of dangerously cool air slammed his back as he strode up to the front door and rang the bell. The storm was close.

His instructions were simple. Ring the bell and then enter. He'd find Mr. Nicolas Cyrnica in the first room to the left of the entrance hall, waiting for him. They would be alone in the house, Master Mind had been assured. He worked better without distractions, especially those distractions from other minds with their emotional needs and mental shouts, clamoring to be heard.

He entered a tiled foyer gaudily furnished with expensive antiques. Nicolas Cyrnica had probably bought everything in sight with the funds he was accused of embezzling from his business partners.

It would have been a dazzling room, with block glass walls on either side of the double front doors and an immense skylight above. The tiled floor was peach-bright. But, the gathering storm darkened the room with a threatening pall. In fact, several hall lamps were on to light the way into the adjoining room where Nicolas waited.

Master Mind had taken his time getting there and paused for a few moments to think over the details of his investigation thus far. He'd left his office in St. Louis yesterday morning and driven across Missouri to Kansas City where he spent the remainder of the day researching his prey. He spent the night there in a rather expensive hotel his clients provided, then after a leisurely and late breakfast, drove southwest out of the city toward this isolated farm.

Mr. Nicolas Cyrnica was from Armenia, a small nation freed during the break-up of the Soviet Union, which hadn't decided if it was part of the Middle East, or an exotic southern extremity of Europe. Nicolas's business partners were for the most part Russians, and there was no love between the two ethnic groups.

Master Mind strode through the open doorway on his left, prepared to face his prey. Dramatically, as if his dark costume and mask were not striking enough, thunder boomed in a long roll outside, loud enough to penetrate the thick walls of the mansion.

"Hello, Mr. Master Mind. Coffee, or tea? Or something stronger?"

If Master Mind had not already poured over half a dozen photos of Nicolas, he would have thought he was confronting the businessman's bodyguard, rather than the man himself. Standing behind a polished oak desk, a hulk of an individual extended a beefy paw for Master Mind to shake.

Taller than even the tall superhero investigator, the Armenian was all muscle. Massive shoulders stretched a tailored yellow-gold tee shirt. Expensive jeans were embellished by a gleaming leather belt and flashy gold buckle. Casual? Filthy rich casual.

Dark brows hovered over golden orbs and darker lashes. Broad, fleshy cheeks were unshaven. Thick lips and a blunt nose overwhelmed the insincere smile with brooding sensuality. Nicolas hadn't bothered shaving for this interview? Strange, arrogant, or carefully contrived?

Master Mind took the hand and shook it firmly. Their eyes met briefly, his cloud-grey ones dancing over the golden Armenian ones before sliding away to take in all the big man's appearance at once.

He looked like a thug, swarthy and physically intimidating. Dark looks, subconsciously equated with evil, overpowered the bright shirt and fake smile. As they shook hands, Master Mind tested the waters before replying to the polite offer of beverage, reaching out with a mere tendril of his mental powers.

What he saw was himself. No surprise, as this would be the dominating image Nicolas Cyrnica currently entertained. Master Mind always dressed in his costume when interviewing suspects. It emphasized his abilities, which nine-tenths of those he met doubted.

Tall, and draped in emerald leather from head to toe, but an emerald so dark it was hard to distinguish from black itself, his mop of auburn hair protruded above his mask in the only splash of muted color other than his pale eyes and bowed, pink lips. He was runner-lean, and had the look of someone who could move very quickly if need be, which was dangerously true. Even his hands were gloved in emerald-opal leather. The lower half of his face was exposed, and his ears, but the mask that obscured his upper face also concealed his identity.

A bulge in the snug-fitting leather pants swelled. The cock beneath stirred and rose to attention.

Master Mind snapped vice-like control over the image, pushing it away as he abandoned his suspect's mind with abrupt surprise. He inhaled sharply and blinked as he released the hand still gripping his and stepped back.

What was that all about? The sexual tension in the room crackled. A single lamp on the desk flickered in the gloom and then went out as lightning struck outside in a blinding flash. Thunder followed immediately.

"The power's gone out. A fucking nuisance. Wouldn't you say?"

The voice was a mimicking rumble, the fake smile still hovering on thick lips that looked very wet. Nicolas Cyrnica licked those lips in the gloomy aftermath of that brilliant flash.

"Yes, a fucking nuisance," Master Mind murmured in reply. Abruptly, he stabbed into the suspect's head, a rough feint he felt necessary under the strange circumstances.

He confronted a very naked Mr. Cyrnica, sprawled over that polished oak desk. Muscular, dark ass cheeks were spread wide. Hefty balls and a swollen dick dangled down below hairy, parted thighs.

"Did my business partners warn you I was a faggot? Did they tell you I like to take cock up the ass? And did they admit that's why they're framing me for embezzlement?"

The words were spoken aloud, and Master Mind held up one gloved hand to silence Nicolas. He broadcast directly into the man's head.

"No more talking. I've advised you over the phone of my abilities. Our interview will be conducted mentally – where lies are hardest to maintain."

Nicolas reared back as if struck in the face. His smirk faltered, but then returned. He was cocky!

Master Mind lunged. "Did you want to take cock up the ass now? Bent over your desk?"

The thrust of lewd thought slammed into Nicolas's startled head. It was his own previous fantasy, in every detail. Nicolas saw himself, his massive, swarthy body, naked and draped over his own desk, waiting for cock.

Master Mind's cock raged under his leather costume. Lightning struck again outside, and thunder rattled the walls. His control slipped, and he blasted into Nicolas's head with the searing image of his hard prick stabbing up between those naked ass cheeks in search of a hot hole.

Momentary darkness followed the brilliant flash. Master Mind blinked, then gasped as he found himself confronting a sprawled Armenian right between his legs. His suspect had leaped over the desk and spun around to drape himself provocatively between Master Mind and his own office furniture.

The fury of the storm arrived like a tsunami. Rain battered the windows in a deluge. Mid-day, it may as well have been deepest twilight. Master Mind could barely see the hulking form in front of him, but felt the heat of muscular thighs pressing back against his own. He had been standing close to the desk, and there was practically no space between him and this unexpected development.

He couldn't help himself, and thrust again into the maelstrom of his suspect's head. Nicolas's clothes were being torn off by emerald-gloved hands. His dark head twisted around to see stiff cock emerging from between silver buttons in a leather fly.

Master Mind broke the connection with a supreme effort. His hands were already moving. He stripped the Armenian with crazed hands. T-shirt was yanked over a dark scalp and tossed aside. Bulging arms and thick back muscles appeared. A deep valley of spine knifed downward to jeans Master Mind tore down while Nicolas himself struggled to help as he writhed against the surface of his own polished desk.

Even if they wanted to speak, the torrent outside would have drowned their words. Master Mind stared down at his handiwork with feverish eyes. A naked ass, hugely muscled, amber flesh lightly coated with a down of black hair, giant thighs below with swirling silky fur barely disguising their powerful bulk. Brawny arms sprawled wide over that polished wood surface.

The ass writhed upwards, the cheeks parted as Nicolas spread his feet wider apart and offered himself, lewdly and obviously.

Master Mind's cock emerged, just as his suspect had imagined it would. He unsnapped the silver buttons of his fly and let loose the thick fuck snake raring to burrow deep between those amber, furry muscle-mounds.

The superhero investigator thrust forward with his hips, his hot cock sliding up into the heated ass crack. His mind thrust forward simultaneously, penetrating Nicolas as surely as that cock was about to penetrate his willing asshole.

A chaos of lust swelled up and outward. As Master Mind rubbed his pre-cum oozing cock-head along the smooth ass crack, Nicolas shivered with desire, feeling that turgid pole searching out his eager butt hole. He ached to be filled with throbbing meat. He wanted to be fucked, impaled, rammed deep.

Master Mind jabbed at the crinkled pucker-hole his dick had settled on. Nicolas responded, squirming back to meet that blunt crown. His asshole quivered and expanded, anal lips opening in a suck-like pulse.

Master Mind read the Armenian thug's thoughts just before the event transpired, hearing the plea as he drove inward.

"I want cock," Nicolas moaned inwardly. "Yes! So hot and so hard and so deep!"

Master Mind thrust with his own thoughts, invading the head as he invaded the asshole.

"I want your steaming hole! I want to fill it with my big cock. I want to fuck it and fuck it."

It was a colliding dance of both inward images and physical reality. Nicolas experienced the wrenching power of cock up his ass and the simultaneous sensation of feeling the opposite – cock experiencing steamy asshole pulsing around it. Inexplicably, Nicolas felt his own ass enveloping Master Mind's cock, that cock being sucked into the vortex of hungry male hole. He was in two worlds at once, his own sensations, and the lusty sensations of the masked investigator fucking him. It rocked Nicolas to the core.

The superhero's pleasure was too intense to contain, bombarding the fucked thug with images of his own asshole being stuffed with hot dick. Nicolas shouted out loud in disbelief, and raw fear, only to have that shriek drowned in the roar of the storm battling against the walls of his mansion.

Master Mind thrust deep. His gloved hands spread open that silken-furred butt, providing a perfect view of his own purple-engorged dick as it drove between puckered ass lips, buried itself, and then pulled back out. He felt steamy hole surround his shaft, and read Nicolas's own nasty thoughts at the same time, feeling his own cock hard and twitching as it penetrated and filled the man's insides.

It was rough, almost to the point of brutal, as Master Mind pounded his cock home, harder and deeper. Yet every thrust was met with mental greed for more of the same, only rougher, more violent and even faster.

Master Mind read his suspect like an open book, knowing when to reach down with one gloved hand and begin pumping the dangling cock that leaked pre-cum in a drool across the polished wood. He teased the oozing slit, expertly reading Nicolas's pleasure even as he pounded ass harder and faster.

Master Mind read the sensations bombarding Nicolas's prostate, which only intensified the aching pleasure along Nicolas's oozing cock as Mastermind's smooth glove-encased fingers stroked and teased it.

The superhero was a madman. He pounded ass, the brawny globes writhing and bucking over the desk top as rain pounded down outside and more lightning struck to blaze the room with brilliance. Any control of the situation had been abandoned in the thrust and pump of aching dick up greedy, sucking asshole. Master Mind reeled in the mental storm, but then latched onto his own inner resolve. Even while riding the savage fuck, he whipped his mind toward the larger goal.

"Why are you embezzling money from your partners? And how much? And what have you done with it all?"

The stab of questions drove into Nicolas's lust-tormented head. The Armenian was like so many others, unwilling to truly believe in this masked man's mental powers, yet was now being confronted with the undeniable reality of those powers. He had no choice but to accept the superhero's dominance.

"I haven't stolen a penny! They're transferring funds from our accounts regularly to their own offshore banks, and blaming me!"

The shouted inner plea didn't fool Master Mind. There was a trick to mind reading. People could actually lie in their heads, sometimes with more ease than telling fibs out loud. They could make anything up; the difference between reality, truth, and fantasy was all a blur in the world of the mind. Master Mind probed deeper.

"How do you know that? You're doing it, too, aren't you?"

Cock slammed hard up asshole. Master Mind's dick was on fire. That quaking asshole clamped and seized his dick with greedy desire. Nicolas's tormented thoughts raged around both his own asshole, and the cock that probed it, all in a chaos of sensations that were unraveling him into tattered shreds of splayed emotions.

The Armenian groaned inwardly as his orgasm approached. Master Mind read it perfectly, thrusting against the writhing man's prostate with mashing intensity while stroking the leaking cock with rapid pumps.

Nicolas drowned in the blend of physical pounding and mental mind-fuck. "Yes! We're all stealing from each other! It's every man for himself! If I don't take as much as I can, the bastards will steal it all before I get my share!"

Master Mind felt the orgasm at the same moment he read it in Nicolas's head. A rush of ecstatic pleasure pulsed like light up from big furry balls and out a pulsing cock. Inside, Nicolas's battered asshole throbbed and clenched in an orgasm of its own, milking the fat cock embedded deep within.

As the super-sleuth felt that release envelop his suspect's body and mind, he inadvertently succumbed to it himself. He didn't cum, but rode along with Nicolas's rapture instead. He pulled his throbbing dick from the convulsing butthole and placed it against one sweaty, quaking asscheek.

He slipped three gloved fingers into the just-fucked hole, feeling the lips open to him completely as Nicolas surrendered to his orgasm. Rather than diminishing, the rapture grew more total. Nicolas felt his own ass lips quiver around the probing fingers, sensed his own inner capitulation to the superhero's powers.

Master Mind's control slipped away as the storm raged outside. He fell into the pit of Nicolas's swirling thoughts as his fingers twisted deep into the pit of Nicolas's hot asshole. He lifted one of the man's brawny thighs up onto the desk and pumped his swollen-oozing cock against the fleshy butt globe, opening up ass crack and asshole to his three gloved fingers.

Nicolas was a man living in a fortress. He ringed himself with defenses against a world he found threatening. His business dealings were a ruthless battlefield, and everyone his enemy. He never emerged from behind those high walls, except when he got fucked.

A hard fuck up the ass was the only time the Armenian gave in. The surrender of his hungry ass to cock was the only experience he relished. Master Mind breathed in steady gasps as he probed that slack hole with his fingers and fucked a powerful ass cheek with his cock. The superhero drowned in Nicolas's surrender.

It was all hole and fingers and oozing cocks. Nicolas's own dick remained hard and twitching even when its load was spent. His asshole remained pliant and hungry, taking three fingers deep inside and bucking up to meet them.

Master Mind read Nicolas's pleasure as if it were his own. He sensed the joy of asshole being probed so expertly and fully. He felt big hard cock rubbing against beefy ass through the avenue of Nicolas's own lewd thoughts.

Master Mind orgasmed.

Cum spewed from his cock slit to coat one hairy ass cheek while fingers dug around inside a willing asshole, and he toppled over the mewling suspect he'd come to interrogate and instead ended up bonding with.

Nicolas stripped Master Mind with shaking hands. He lay on his back across his own desk and raised his beefy thighs for a second round of cock up the ass, staring at Master Mind's lean, athletic body and exposed face, seeing the man behind the hero like no other had been allowed to.

Master Mind fucked Nicolas just as violently the second time, both their needs multiplying and expanding as they opened up to each other more deeply than either had expected or even wanted.

The beefy thighs pulled back to hairy muscular chest that heaved with lust. The ass crack was wide open, the heated hole pink and swollen from steady fucking. Nicolas was as open as he possibly could be to that stabbing fuck weapon. Master Mind was totally naked, no costume to protect him from the chaos of his own powers.

Truth and lies sorted themselves out as the rainstorm intensified, threatened them with imminent destruction as a tornado passed within mere miles, then diminished as both men orgasmed with wracking power for the second time.

The maelstrom of storm and mutual orgasm settled into a rocking, naked embrace over Nicolas's polished desk.

Nicolas gazed up at soft grey eyes and attempted a smile. He still looked like a thug, with those heavy brows, liquid eyes and blunt features. But it was only a facade. "Do you understand why I've done it? Can't you see those guys deserve to be ripped off? They're thieves. Stealing from thieves can't really be wrong, can it?"

"There is a difference between right and wrong, Mr. Cyrnica. I don't think I have to tell you that."

"What about good and bad? It's not all black and white, you know. People are complicated."

It sounded like Nicolas was making the usual excuses all Master Mind's suspects dredged up when caught in their crimes. But there was more. The superhero had seen deeper, not for the first time, but for the first time in that gut-wrenching, intimate way.

Master Mind grinned. "I'm duty bound to make my report, and I won't lie for you." Seeing the look of hurt in the brooding eyes, the superhero quickly continued. "But I will offer to take your case, too. How about I stick around a few days, and you give me all the dirt on your partners? That way I can present it to them as a package."

Nicolas finished the thought for Master Mind. "They won't be able to go after me when they're just as guilty."

Their eyes met, and for another moment, Master Mind allowed himself to delve beyond those dark orbs. What he saw were visions of upended ass, cock plowing deep and hard, moans of pleasure, and romps in nearly every room of the palatial country home.

"I think you need to work on your image a little," Master Mind said with a smile, glancing around at the ostentatious surroundings.

"Maybe you can help me out."

There was more in those eyes, but Master Mind chose not to pry. Time enough to discover how much more dwelled in that complicated head. Time enough to finally let someone in, even though it was the most unlikely of individuals.

Nicolas reached between their naked bodies and stroked the superhero's stiffening dick. "You can't pick the ones you fall for, can you, Master Mind?"

They shared a laugh as the superhero wondered how much more he and Nicolas would be sharing.

The Bat and The Raven
By Stephen Osborne

Mark Marshall, once the dark blue tights came on, was no longer Mark Marshall. He became The Bat, fighter for justice and niceness everywhere. True, there had been some difficulties at the beginning of his crime-fighting career. The original design for his costume had a design of a full moon on his chest with a fluttering bat silhouette superimposed over it. Unfortunately, he quickly learned (by way of a nasty letter from a team of lawyers) that another superhero, in another city, had a very similar outfit. In order to avoid an expensive lawsuit he could ill afford, Mark re-designed his insignia. Now the moon bore the face of a bat over it. He'd thought this a good compromise until the day a purse-snatcher asked him why he had a picture of a squirrel on his chest. Mark had felt depressed over that, although breaking the villain's jaw had helped.

Other trials followed. Recently, an Hispanic neighbor kid, a cocky boy named Juan Martinez, had discovered Mark's secret identity. Luckily, the eighteen-year-old wanted to become a superhero as well, so Mark took the lad under his wing (so to speak) and trained him. Months of training ensued, and finally Mark declared the boy fit for battle. The boy chose a tight fitting black outfit, complete with black cape, black boots, and face-mask and decided to call himself The Raven. A yellow-beaked bird with evil red eyes adorned The Raven's chest plate.

"We're going to make an unbeatable combination," the boy growled excitedly, smashing his fist against his other palm.

The Bat had to agree. He nearly forgot his gruff persona for a moment and told Juan that he'd like to be a combination in another way as well, but he knew he couldn't. While gay superheroes did exist, (Super Bruce down in Sydney came immediately to mind) they certainly weren't the norm. No, superheroes were supposed to be tough, heterosexual bastards. Mark would just have to keep his growing feelings for Juan to himself.

Months of the partnership passed, and The Bat and The Raven became feared by the criminal element of Indianapolis. The Bat kept up his persona in front of The Raven fairly well. A glitch occurred once during a training session, when Mark was showing Juan some close-combat drills. The boy at one point managed to get behind Mark and yanked him into a fierce bearhug. The move gave Mark an immediate erection. He had to stop the training session at that point, telling a disappointed Juan that he'd developed a migraine.

I can't let The Raven know how I feel, The Bat told himself.

He contented himself with an active masturbation regimen, usually envisioning a hot wrestling match with the youth, which usually ended up with The Raven giving The Bat the fuck of his life.

That was another reason The Bat could never reveal his true self. How could anyone respect The Bat as a formidable crime-fighting force if they knew he was, in fact, a nelly bottom?

The Raven had been begging The Bat to let him tackle a case himself. "I want to show you what I can do," Juan told him. Mark tried not to look into those big, brown, dreamy eyes. "I want to let you know how much I've learned."

When the call came in that the bank on Tenth and Meridian was being robbed, The Bat agreed to let The Raven do all the fighting. "I'll just observe," he told the boy.

They caught up with the robbers in the alley behind the bank. True to his word, The Bat kept to the shadows and let his young partner beat the crap out of the two miscreants. The Raven eagerly jumped in front of the two men, a crooked smile on his face. "Not so fast," he said. "You're forgetting something."

One of the robbers frowned. "What's that?"

"This!" The boy's right leg kicked out, smashing into the guy's stomach. With a loud "Ooof!" the man went down. The Raven turned to other villain, neatly kicking the gun out of the man's hand.

The Bat watched, his excitement growing, as The Raven proceeded to make mincemeat out of his opponents. Anyone else seeing the action in the dark alley would have a hard time making out the movements of The Raven, as his jet-black tights made him blend almost seamlessly into the shadows, but The Bat could see his partner's bulging muscles every time the boy slammed a fist into one of the villains. The Bat had good night vision, and besides, he was used to watching The Raven fight.

The second robber reeled from The Raven's right fist, falling noisily back into a garbage can. He shook his head angrily and started to get back up.

"You really don't want to do that," the Raven snarled, kicking out with his right foot. The blow connected with the man's jaw with a loud crack. The Bat smiled as he saw the thief's eyes roll upwards before he slumped, out cold, amid the fallen garbage.

When the first attacker rose again to resume his fight with The Raven, The Bat nearly called out a warning. He stopped himself. He promised the boy that he wouldn't interfere and that this would be The Raven's fight alone. Besides, the boy was on top of things. He spun quickly and smacked the ruffian with a hard right to the jaw.

He's so good, The Bat thought to himself. *He fights like a tiger. I love to watch his lithe, strong body as he pummels the crap out of idiots like these. His taut muscles showing up so well in those black tights. The funny way he grunts as he kicks a bad guy in the stomach. The way those beautiful dark eyes shine as his black-gloved fist connects with some villain's teeth....*

The Bat tried to stop his train of thought, but it was too late. Already, his swelling cock was straining against the tight fabric of his midnight blue outfit. If he couldn't get it to subside within the next few minutes, The Raven would finish with his opponent and might catch sight of his mentor watching him with an obvious woody. The one major drawback to wearing tights was that erections showed up extremely well. It wouldn't do to have The Raven see his stiffy. That wouldn't do at all. The young man looked up to him. Maybe if he stepped behind the dumpster, he could quickly take care of the problem. A few strokes and there wouldn't be anything for the Raven to see. The Bat moved into the shadows, his hand already fumbling to get into his shorts.

He found a spot out of sight of the action. Yanking his tights down to release his swollen dick, The Bat risked looking over the dumpster to watch the fight. He pumped his cock, watching as The Raven lifted the ruffian up off the ground by his shirt collar. The boy hauled back and rammed a hard right across the guy's jaw. That was all it took. The man was out like a light.

That was all it took for The Bat as well. As The Raven stood victorious over his fallen foes, The Bat shot a huge load. He had to bite his lip to keep from calling out as cum gushed from his dick. Most of it hit the dumpster, but one large glob fell and splattered on his thigh.

Great, The Bat thought. Like a white stain isn't going to be obvious on midnight blue tights.

He managed to pull his shorts back up just as The Raven walked over to him. The boy was smiling broadly. "What did you think?"

The Bat gulped. He tried unsuccessfully to keep his voice from shaking as he replied, "Um ... fine. It was just ... fine. I especially like the spinning back kick you gave that guy. Nearly knocked his head off. Very good. Excellent, in fact."

The Raven beamed with pleasure. "It means a lot to me to hear you say that." His eyes narrowed. "Are you OK?

You seem a little out of breath. I'm the one that was kicking ass, not you. Hey, you've got something on your leg, by the way."

Embarrassed, The Bat brushed at the stain. "Yeah," he said. "A pigeon went overhead. It shit on my leg. Those damn night pigeons, you know how they are."

"A night pigeon, eh?" The Raven seemed about to say something else, but a sound in the alley behind them made him jump. "What the hell was that?"

A figure emerged from the shadows. Dressed in his usual green tights, the villain known as The Crackler laughed as he stood in front of the heroic duo. Pointing his electrified cane in their direction, The Crackler snorted. "If Dim-Bird here swallows the night pigeon story, he'll have to turn himself in to the Audubon Society for examination. I may be a Supervillain and possibly the most evil person in the state of Indiana with the exception of the Governor, but at least I know a cum stain when I see one."

"You take that back, you vile villain!" The Raven sputtered.

"Nice alliteration there, chum," The Bat said.

The Raven blushed slightly at the compliment. "Thanks, Bat."

The Crackler shook his head in disbelief. "Touching. Very touching. I almost wish I didn't have to kill the two of you. You'd make a nice couple otherwise. Unfortunately, it states clearly in the Supervillain charter that I've got to do my best to destroy you utterly, and that's what I'm here to do!" With that the Crackler lunged forward, swatting The Bat's shoulder with his electric cane.

The pain that shot through The Bat was excruciating. He slumped to his knees, holding his shoulder. His eyes blurred from the shock, but he still saw The Raven leap into action.

"You can't do that to him!" the boy shouted, kicking up with terrifying force. His boot smashed into The Crackler's jaw, knocking the man backwards. The cane flew from his grasp. Before the villain could react, The Raven was on him. The boy pelted the Crackler with rights and lefts, screaming, "No one gets the best of The Bat! That man is everything to me!"

His eyesight clearing, The Bat could see the Crackler's surprise at the ferocity of The Raven's attack. "Hey!" he shouted in between punches from The Raven. "Lighten up! I'm supposed to hurt the bastard! That's what Supervillains do!"

"Yeah?" The Raven snarled. "Well, this is what The Raven does, and I hope it hurts!" He spun in the air, his boot smashing savagely against the Crackler's head. The villain collapsed, unconscious.

Sirens sounded in the distance. "The police can clean this mess up," The Raven said, helping The Bat back to his feet. "Let me get you home."

"I'm fine now," The Bat protested. "The effect from his cane has passed."

"Nonsense. You're hurt. Let's get back to the Bat Pad."

The Bat Pad was, in fact, just an ordinary suburban home, but a Superhero couldn't just say, "Let's get back to 944 Summit Drive." It lacked panache.

Entering the house, Mark (he'd taken off his mask, so he was Mark again) expected the lad to lead him to his bedroom to recuperate, but instead Juan led him to the spare room, the one with the wrestling mat where they held their training sessions. "What are we doing here?" he asked.

"You're sure you're OK?" the boy asked.

"One hundred percent," Mark replied only seconds before the boy slapped a crushing bear hug onto him. He grunted and strained, but couldn't break the hold.

"Remember this?" Juan asked, a hint of laughter in his voice.

Mark would have replied, but the young man's muscular grip was making it hard to breathe. He grunted as his protégé lifted him up off his feet. The hold tightened. Mark struggled to no avail. As before, his dick hardened at the handsome Hispanic nearly crushed his ribs. Suddenly, The Raven brought his lips close to Mark's ear.

"You give?" he asked.

"I give," The Bat grunted. He immediately regretted the words. What would happen when Juan released the hold and witnessed his enormous stiffy? The partnership would be over, and Mark wasn't sure he could deal with life without The Raven.

The young man let him go only to wrestle him to the mat. Mark yelped as he hit the floor, although he enjoyed feeling the weight of Juan on top of him. If only …

The black clad boy pinned him, all the while sporting a huge grin. Mark let his eyes wander just for a second and saw that The Raven bore a large bulge as well, straining to be released from the tights. The youngster laughed and gave Mark's crotch a rub. "Shall we?" he asked.

The Bat couldn't believe his ears. "What do you mean?"

Juan chuckled and pulled Mark's tights down, allowing his large cock to spring out. "You do want me to fuck you, don't you?" he asked as he struggled to yank his own tights down.

Mark couldn't believe his ears. "How did you know?"

"I've known since I saw your eyes the first time I kicked a guy in the face. You like watching my muscles. And that's cool because I like you, too. So much that I want to fuck you." Without waiting for an answer, Juan used his hand to guide the tip of his cock to Mark's waiting ass. Mark shifted, throwing his legs over the boy's shoulders. He gazed into the young man's deep, soulful eyes and winced only slightly as Juan's cock entered him.

It was just as he'd always imagined it would be. The Raven, still mostly in costume, slammed his dick hard into The Bat's ass. Mark moan with pleasure and reached down to play with his own aching cock. They gazed into each others eyes and both of them smiled.

"Just one thing," Juan said, panting each time he thrust his cock home.

"Yeah?" Mark asked.

"The billing. Instead of The Bat and The Raven, it should be ..." Juan paused as a groan forced its way out of his throat. He began fucking The Bat harder, obviously close to climax. Finally he could speak again. "It should be The Raven and The Bat. The top should get top billing."

Mark grinned with pleasure. "No problem," he said as he felt Juan shoot his wad inside him.

A Dirty Job
By Kiernan Kelly

Thunderous explosions rocked the foundation of the building as thick black clouds of smoke roiled up into the leaden sky, belched free from windows aglow with red and orange flame. With a metallic scream, the sign that had proclaimed the building to be the Hathaway House Orphanage popped its rivets, tearing free and crashing to the street below, splintering on impact.

A woman screamed and pointed to the fifth floor of the building, the only floor not yet engulfed in flame. There, framed in one of the soot-blackened windows of the orphanage, a small child in a thin white nightdress stood teetering on the narrow ledge. Flames licked up toward her feet from the floor below, her pitiful screams swallowed by the roar of the inferno.

Suddenly, a deep voice boomed from the rooftop of the building directly across the street from the raging fire, commanding the attention of everyone for blocks around. "Fear not! I'll save you!"

Heads snapped up just in time to see the figure of a man leap headfirst from the roof, his thickly muscled body poured into bright blue latex. His red cape fluttered in his wake as he soared through the air in defiance of physics, sweeping the child off the ledge a heartbeat before the room behind her exploded into flame.

Amid the cheering of the crowd, Perfecto executed a flawless one-point landing on the sidewalk with the girl cradled safely in the crook of his powerful arm. An errant breeze lifted tendrils of his blonde, shoulder length hair as he smiled a perfect, white, shining grin that deepened the dimples in his strong, square jaw. Cameras flashed, their lights making his cerulean eyes twinkle.

"Fuck me," Louie grumbled as he tossed an empty can of Miller Light at the television screen. "Dirk got another one! How many does that make this week? Seven?"

"He's good," Jack replied as he ran a hot iron repeatedly over a minute wrinkle that stubbornly refused to lay flat on his green cape. As the Cloaked Champion, he was first to admit that he was rather anal about his cape.

"Bullshit. I'm willing to bet that the only reason he gets these cake assignments is because he's blowing the Chief," Louie argued peevishly. He stood up, scratching his belly under his stained, yellowed wife beater. Standing just a hair over six feet, Louie had barely made the height requirement for superhero. His boyish good looks and wavy blue-black hair had made him seem perfect for the job, however, as had his cockeyed grin. The fact that he fit the costume hadn't hurt either, and he'd gotten the job as Electroman. Now, ten years later, he still looked good – if he didn't stand too closely to Dirk, who was known to the rest of the peons of the world as Perfecto.

"You're just jealous, Louie. If you'd get your ass out of that recliner once in a while and go down to Headquarters, maybe you'd get a few more choice assignments," Jack chided. He lifted his cape off the ironing board and grimaced at the triangular scorch mark that had burned smack dab in the middle of it. "I got that rescue last week, didn't I?"

"Rescue? You call that a rescue? You got to get a fucking cat out of a tree, Jack. And you only got that assignment because the Fire Department was too busy responding to a gas leak over on 33rd. The very same gas leak, might I remind you, that Dirk drew as his assignment!"

"It was still a rescue, wasn't it? What was the last assignment that you got, Louie? I have no idea because I can't fucking remember back that far!" Jack snipped, frowning. He tossed his scorched cape around his shoulders, fastening it at his throat.

"You know that it's true, Jack. Ever since Dirk and his pretty-boy friends showed up, the rest of us have been reduced to nothing more than glorified crossing guards. It's pathetic! The Chief is only concerned about how well they photograph. He's turned into a goddamn publicity whore. He doesn't give a rat's ass about the rest of us, the poor schmucks who were the backbone of the Organization for so many years!" Louie ranted, pacing back and forth across the living room rug. "When was the last time you saw Supersonic Man or Octoclops on the seven o'clock news?" He narrowed his eyes at the television screen, which was replaying the daring rescue at the fire scene for the third time. On the screen, Dirk again saved the girl, and again the crowd went wild.

"Suck my hairy fucking balls, you dick-headed wanker!" Louis shouted, pointing his finger at the television. The images sputtered and flipped for a moment before the screen went black and a thin wisp of smoke curled up lazily from the back of the set.

"Goddamn it, Louie! That's the fourth set you've fried in the last two months. You need to get over this and realize that sometimes saving the world is a dirty job. We can't always get the high-profile gigs. Sometimes being a superhero means having to save a cat from a tree. Look, I'm going down to the bar to get a drink. Why don't you hose yourself off and come with me?" Jack asked. "You're so fucking ripe you could add 'Paralyzing Pit Reek' to your list of superpowers."

"Bite me."

* * * * *

Wedged between a bodega and a boarded-over haberdashery, the Hero Worship Bar was a rundown hole-in-the-wall with a faded green awning outside and a jukebox that skipped continuously inside.

Four men, dressed in colorful spandex bodysuits and shiny patent leather boots, sat at the battered bar under a flickering Budweiser neon sign. If one looked closely enough – although one would risk getting zapped with a lightning bolt up one's ass if one tried – one would see the worn spots at the knees of their tights and the scorch marks on their capes.

"It's just not fair. Whatever happened to seniority? We were fighting Supervillains and saving the world while they were still shitting their diapers," Louis continued to grumble as the bartender slopped a mug of beer down in front of him, spraying his lap with foam.

"Louie's got a point, Jack," Larry, a.k.a. Octoclops said, reaching for a fistful of peanuts from the bowl that sat on the bar, "Maybe we should unionize." Six of his eight eyes were focused on Jack, but the other two were eyeballing the tall, powerfully built blonde who had just entered the bar. "Don't look now, but the hero of the hour just walked in."

Three of the superheroes immediately ducked their heads down over their beers. "Damn it! Don't make eye contact, Octo. Don't … aww, shit it's too late. Here he comes," Louie moaned, sighing so hard that he blew the head off of his beer as Dirk beamed his high-wattage smile at them and ambled in their direction.

"Gentlemen! I trust you're all feeling super?" Dirk said, throwing his head back and laughing heartily, oblivious to the pained groans of the other caped crusaders.

It was what Dirk always said each and every time he saw them, and it grated on their nerves like fingernails on a chalkboard. They muttered a collective, "Yeah, super … ha, ha," with all the enthusiasm of road-kill.

The barkeep carefully placed a large, frosty mug of beer in front of Dirk without spilling a single drop, and slid the peanuts out from under Larry's hand to within Dirk's reach. "Nice save you made today, Dirk!" he said, nearly drooling.

Not even Louie could blame the bartender for falling over himself trying to serve Dirk. As much as Louie would have loved to see Dirk dipped in chocolate, rolled in walnuts and fed to the nearest herd of wild hogs, he had to admit that Dirk was nothing if not drool-worthy.

Dirk topped the six-six mark easily, and that wasn't even counting his thick mane of golden hair. His bright blue eyes matched the color of his superhero costume perfectly. A strong, chiseled jaw was sculpted by just the right amount of five o'clock shadow, and his cheeks creased with two deep dimples when he smiled. And that smile! All those lovely, straight white teeth gleaming all at once were nearly enough to blind a man, if a man happened to be looking at his smile. No one did, of course. They were all always too busy staring at the oversized bulge at Dirk's crotch to notice his teeth. Louie would have loved to believe that Dirk stuffed it, but something told him that that would be wishful thinking. No, Dirk was real, every inch of him. Every foot of him, Louie corrected himself as he let his gaze wander over Dirk's impressive package.

Clearly outlined under his tight superhero Speedo, Dirk's cock was at least as thick as Louie's wrist and nearly as long as his forearm. That it was also always fully erect didn't help matters. To the casual observer, it looked as though Dirk had a long, fat crowbar wedged in his crotch.

To add insult to injury, Dirk was every bit as gorgeous going as he was coming. The twin mounds of steel that served him as an ass moved fluidly, hypnotically, under his spandex briefs, revealed when his cape swished side to side with each roll of his lean hips. Begrudgingly, Louis conceded that Dirk probably didn't need to lift a finger to stop a Supervillain – all he had to do was show up, and the villains would handcuff themselves for his convenience.

"Louie? Louie!" Jack growled, shoving a not-too-subtle elbow into Louie's side, trying to get his attention. "Dirk was asking us if we'd like to go to a party."

"Party? What party?" Louie repeated, still struggling to tear his eyes away from the steel girder that was straining the fabric between Dirk's heavily muscled thighs.

"It's a little get-together the Chief is throwing for me in honor of my one year anniversary of fighting crime," Dirk grinned, blushing just enough to look boyishly endearing. "I'd love for the old gang to be there."

"Old? Who are you calling old?" Supersonic Man, known to his friends as Phil, growled.

"No, no, that's not what I meant, Phil. I meant the original gang, the ones I looked up to as a boy," Dirk explained, patting Phil on the shoulder and nearly knocking him off of his stool.

Louie's mind whirled even though his eyes remained super-glued to Dirk's crotch. A devious grin slanted his lips as a plan quickly formulated in his brain, and he nodded. "Sure, we'd love to be there, right boys?"

"Uh, but Louie, didn't you just say that Dirk and ..." Larry said, all eight of his eyes blinking in confusion.

"I said that we'd love to go. Isn't that what I just said, Jack?" Louie interrupted, hoping that Jack would be a little quicker on the uptake than Larry.

Thankfully, he was. "Oh, uh ... sure, Louie ... yeah, we'd love to go."

"Great!" Dirk boomed, his deep voice sending a tremor though the glasses and bottles behind the bar and through every groin in the room. "See you tomorrow night at eight, over at the Majestic Ballroom." He grinned and waved, then turned and sauntered out of the bar with every eye in the joint riveted on his firm, spandex-coated ass.

No sooner had the door shut behind him that a half-dozen hands and as many furious questions smacked Louie simultaneously.

"Are you insane? What the fuck were you thinking, Louie?" Larry asked, frowning. "You were just complaining that he strolled into Headquarters and took over, getting all the juicy assignments, and now you want us to go help the biggest offender celebrate his success?"

"Yeah, Louie! Are you nuts?" Phil added, folding his arms across his chest, staring hard at Louie.

"Come on, Louie ... give. I know that there's something going on in that melon you call a head. What's the plan?" Jack asked, narrowing his eyes at his friend.

"There's a plan?" Larry asked in confusion, his eyebrows arching over his eyes like eight bushy caterpillars. "What plan?"

"Of course there's a plan! An ingenious one, if I do say so myself," Louie replied. "It's simple. We go to the party and make nice with everyone – especially Dirk and his buddies. We play to their egos. We fetch them drinks. We dance with them. We kiss their collective narcissistic asses. And then, once we're in good with them, we can find out what their weaknesses are, and ... bingo! No more Big Mister Perfecto. Things can go back to the way they used to be before he showed up."

"That's it. You've finally lost what little bit of a mind you had left, Louie! I know it's been a while since you last fought evil, but what you're suggesting is what villains do, not heroes. We're the good guys, remember?" Jack said, flicking his finger against the tip of Louie's nose.

"Relax," Louie said, swatting Jack's hand away from his face. "We aren't going to kill them – we're just going to keep them on a shorter leash," Louie argued. "Especially Dirk. If we know what his weakness is, then we can use that knowledge to get him to stand down once in a while and let us have a shot at getting some of the better assignments."

Jack's mouth slowly turned up in a knowing smile, and he sat back, eyeing Louie with awe. "Brilliant. Underhanded and manipulative, but brilliant," he said. "I hate to say it, but it just might work!"

"Of course it will work," Louie grinned. "Dirk is fucked ... he just doesn't know it yet."

* * * * *

The Majestic Ballroom was suitably named. It was an immense, high-domed room glittering with glass, brass, and class. From the massive chandeliers that dripped Swarovski crystal and the gleaming Italian marble floors to the full, sixteen-piece tuxedoed orchestra, the place literally screamed money and privilege.

Louie hated it on sight.

The room swarmed with the upper rungs of society; rich and cultured people whom Louie had never met, and who certainly didn't give a flying fuck about him. For his one-year anniversary, the Chief had given him a stale doughnut and a cup of vending machine coffee. And yet, for Dirk the Magnificent, the Chief had hired out the most expensive place in town. Louie's gut roiled with the injustice of it all.

The Majestic's only saving grace, as far as Louie was concerned, was the vast buffet table that ran along one entire side of the room. Laden with every type of delicacy Louie could imagine, the caviar alone probably cost more than Louie and his friends had seen lumped together in one place in their lifetimes. Already, Supersonic Man was nearly hidden behind a plate piled high with jumbo shrimp, Octoclops was endeavoring to eat his weight in pâté de foie gras, and the Cloaked Champion was drowning himself in the lobster bisque soup.

"You three latch yourselves onto Dirk's pals," Louie whispered as he popped a decadent dark chocolate-covered strawberry into his mouth, "and I'll get after Dirk. Compliment them. Stroke their egos. Stroke anything they want stroked for that matter, just make sure you get the information about their weaknesses. We'll meet back here in two hours."

Jack, Phil, and Larry nodded, their mouths so full of food that their cheeks bulged like cartoon chipmunks. Louie rolled his eyes and shook his head, then searched the room for Dirk.

Perfecto wasn't difficult to find. All Louie had to do was determine where the crowd was the thickest, the laughter the loudest, and the drool the deepest before he found Dirk, dead center in the middle of it, basking in the admiration of his peers. He shouldered his way into the crowd until he stood so close to him that Louie could practically taste the champagne Dirk was drinking.

"Oh, hey!" Dirk grinned after Louie had accidentally-on-purpose slammed a foot down on top of Dirk's size eighteen boots to get his attention. "Everyone, you remember Electroman?"

There were hesitant, polite nods from Dirk's circle of admirers, and Louie wanted to zap each and every one of them. *Ding, fries are done,* he thought, picturing them all fried and frazzled and slightly blackened around the edges. He pushed the thought out of his mind and concentrated on Dirk.

For a while, Louie worked hard to make himself indistinguishable from anyone else in the We Love Dirk Fan Club. He laughed at Dirk's jokes, praised his daring rescues; he nodded his head at Dirk's sage advice, and did everything short of falling to his knees and licking Dirk's red leather boots. But then a strange thing happened. He found that standing so close to Dirk in all his blonde, heavily muscled, crotch-bulging splendor for so long a time was discombobulating. For a moment, Louie actually forgot the master plan. It was almost as though Dirk was the mothership and Louie was caught in his tractor beam, helplessly being sucked ever deeper into Dirk's orbit. If he didn't do something soon, Louie feared he'd find himself crossing over to the dark side, becoming a dyed in the wool Dirk-worshiper and completely forgetting his purpose in coming to the Majestic Ballroom in the first place.

He couldn't – wouldn't – let that happen. Standing on his tiptoes, Louie whispered into Dirk's ear. "Dirk, I have something really important to ask you. Could we go somewhere a bit more private?" he asked. "The fate of the world hangs in the balance."

"Sure," Dirk answered, nodding his head and looking concerned. "Excuse us for a moment," he said to the crowd around them. He led Louie out of the Ballroom and down a lushly carpeted hallway to an empty office. Closing the door behind them – actually he set the door behind them, having had to rip the locked door off its hinges to get them into the office in the first place – Dirk turned to Louie with a questioning look in his eyes.

Louie swallowed hard and took a deep breath, steeling himself to go in for the kill and find out the truth about Dirk's weakness. A superhero's weakness was his most closely guarded secret. There was only one way Louie knew of to force a man to spill such a secret, and that was by getting him to spill something else first. He stood again on his tiptoes, placed his hands on either side of Dirk's strong-jawed face and crushed his lips against Dirk's.

He felt resistance in Dirk's petal-soft, full lips, but Louie staunchly continued to grind his own against them, thrusting his tongue between them and invading Dirk's mouth with the power and single-minded purpose of a conquering army. His fingers twisted in Dirk's shoulder-length blonde hair, and he ground his groin relentlessly against the steel-like bulge in Dirk's tights. Absently, Louie realized that Dirk's aforementioned bulge was definitely real, every glorious inch of it. Not only was it real, it was as hard as steel and as hot as magma, scalding Louie through the thin fabric of their tights. Louie's cock roared to life, straining against the constricting spandex of his briefs, desperately seeking contact with Dirk's searing iron erection.

"Louie, stop! I can't," Dirk moaned, pushing Louie away with enough force to send a non-superhero hurtling through the wall on the opposite side of the room. As it was, he rocked Louie on his feet and caused him to stumble back an inch or two.

"Why?" Louie growled, "Because I'm not pretty enough for you? Not famous enough?"

"No, that's not it. I want to ... I just can't," Dirk whined, running his hands through his hair as he leaned back against the wall. A thin layer of perspiration dotted his brow, something Louie had never before seen happen to a superhero. They never broke a sweat – ever.

"Then, why not? Come on, Dirk ... you're as hard as a rock," he purred, reaching out and sliding his hand over

Dirk's rigid bulge. A single spot of wetness darkened the blue fabric under his fingers. "You know that you want me. Admit it."

Dirk groaned, twisting his pelvis away from Louie's touch. "Come on, Louie! Stop it. Please."

Louie was beginning to get irritated. "Playing hard to get doesn't suit you, Dirk." He eyed Dirk and watched a drop of sweat drip down the side of his face. Realizing that Dirk was struggling to hold back, he quickly changed tactics. "Want me to tell you what I want to do to you?" he whispered seductively. "I want to strip you naked and run my tongue all over you. I want taste every fucking inch of you. I want to suck on your cock, your balls, and tongue-fuck your asshole until you're squirming and begging me to fuck you," he murmured, running his hands up over Dirk's broad chest. He felt Dirk's nipples pop up under his fingertips, and smiled. "Do you want me to fuck you, Dirk? Pry open your cheeks and lick your asshole, then ram my meat into it until my balls slap against your ass?" He reached around Dirk's hip and dug a single finger into the spandex that covered Dirk's crack.

"Yes!" Dirk roared, "Goddamn it, yes! I can't fucking stand it anymore!" Dirk's eyes were glowing with a need so strong that the force of it nearly knocked Louie off his feet. Dirk took hold of the neckline of his own bodysuit and tore it open to his crotch, exposing a broad expanse of silky, golden skin and two rose-colored, pebbled nipples.

Louie stared at Dirk's ripped pectorals and ridged belly the torn fabric revealed, letting his fingers trail down over them to Dirk's crotch. Taking hold of the material of Dirk's tights, he pulled them down to the tops of his boots with one smooth movement, freeing Dirk's cock of the clinging cloth. *Holy Cum Gun, he's bigger than I even imagined!* Louie thought in awe, as he dropped to his knees before Dirk. *I may have to dislocate my jaw like a fucking snake to get my mouth around him.* He licked his lips then eagerly opened his mouth as wide as he could, his jaws cracking with the effort.

It was like getting mouth-fucked by a lamppost.

Dirk plunged his cock into Louie's mouth so hard that Louie feared it would smash through the back of his throat and out the other side. It filled Louie's mouth completely, a thick, hot dowel of flesh that brushed between his molars and jammed itself deeply down his throat, cutting off Louie's breath. Dirk's hips rocked, and Louie thought frantically that if Dirk's dick forced itself down Louie's throat any deeper it would come out of his ass, virtually fucking him from the inside out. Dirk's balls, two fuzzy, baseball-sized boulders, repeatedly hit Louie in the chin hard enough to leave a mark. He tried to suck on the velvet skin of Dirk's cock, but it was wedged inside of his mouth too tightly for him have much effect. His tongue soaked up Dirk's taste like a sponge – musky, male, and slightly salty with loads of precum.

Finally, the need to breathe became overwhelming, and Louie pulled away from Dirk's molten monster over Dirk's protests, gulping for air. He waited until his lips finally lost their blue, oxygen-deprived tint and his lungs filled with enough air to speak. "On your knees, Dirk. My turn," Louie ordered gruffly, shrugging out of his bodysuit and pulling down his spandex shorts. His cock, while not in the same league as Dirk's, was still impressive enough. Ramrod straight and heavily veined, its rounded head glistened with a few drops of pearly moisture. Louie curled his fist around it, stroking it slowly as he waited for Dirk to comply with his order.

He didn't have long to wait. Dirk dropped down onto all fours almost instantly, presenting his firm ass for Louie's viewing pleasure. A tan line followed the outline of his briefs, his asscheeks glowing white against the rest of Dirk's tawny skin. A fine dusting of light brown hair peeked from the crack that ran between the two pale half moons, and as Dirk lowered his head down to the floor, they parted, giving Louie a peek at Dirk's puckered pink asshole.

Louie dove headfirst between Dirk's ivory cheeks, crazily licking and lapping at the ridged muscle that ringed

Dirk's rectum, slurping loudly. Dirk's moans and frantic wiggling spurred him on, and he thrust his tongue deeply into Dirk's asshole, fucking him until Louie's prediction came true, and Dirk was begging for his cock.

"Fuck me, Louie! Now! Now, goddamn it!" Dirk bellowed, smashing a frustrated fist onto the floor, punching a hole into the carpeted concrete.

Louie took the hint. Fumbling with a condom he'd had tucked into the waistband of his briefs (always be prepared being the slogan of Boy Scouts and Superheroes), he rolled it down over his cock and thrust himself into Dirk's ass in one fell swoop. He buried himself in Dirk's fiery ass, pushing himself in until his pubic hair brushed Dirk's asscheeks. Feeling as though his cock was going to be incinerated by the intense heat of Dirk's rectum as it constricted tightly around his length, Louie pumped himself in and out of Dirk's sweet ass in frenzied thrusts.

His groin was slapping against Dirk's flesh loudly with each plunge, and his climax was beginning to boil up in his gut when Dirk suddenly screamed. Dirk's asshole clenched so tightly around Louie's cock as he came that Louie lost all control and spouted a gusher of his own.

Wave after wave of ecstasy washed over Louie, the blood in his ears drowning out everything but the fireworks that were exploding all around him. The air crackled with static electricity, and every hair on his body stood on end as little blue lightning bolts flashed all around him. Louie emptied himself of what seemed to him to be buckets of semen, shooting a load that would drown an elephant. He hoped that the condom he'd used was capable of holding it all and wouldn't explode like an over-filled water balloon.

Collapsing on top of Dirk, Louie's weight brought them both down flat onto the floor and the ocean of semen that Dirk had flooded the carpet with as he'd climaxed. Breathing hard, they lay there one atop the other, with Louie's softening cock still wedged between Dirk's pale asscheeks.

Eventually, Louie caught his breath and rolled off Dirk. He discarded the condom (thankfully still intact, although barely), and rubbed Dirk's broad shoulders, noticing that they still trembled with the force of Dirk's orgasm. Louie silently congratulated himself on his performance and dragged himself up to a sitting position next to Dirk.

"Oh, God, that was amazing. I can't fucking move," Dirk moaned, trying to lift himself up off the sodden carpet. He managed to raise himself about a half-inch off the floor before falling back facedown with a grunt.

"Come on, get up. We need to do something about your costume before you go back out to your admiring public," Louie chuckled, fingering the torn edges of Dirk's bodysuit. In the aftermath of his incredible orgasm, the entire reason that he'd seduced Dirk in the first place completely slipped his mind. "Unless you're into exhibitionism."

"Can't move."

"Come on, you big lazy lug. Get up," Louie laughed, tugging on a hank of Dirk's hair.

"Can't."

"What do you mean, you can't? Just get up," Louie frowned, poking Dirk on the shoulder. "You can't lay there forever."

"Can't."

Louie looked hard at the back of Dirk's head. Dirk wasn't moving a muscle. Not even a twitch, even though he was lying facedown on a soggy, cum-drenched carpet, a less than comfortable position to be in.

Suddenly, a light went off over Louie's head. In his mind's eye, he saw Dirk on the news, perched on the edge of the building before he'd saved the girl at the orphanage the day before. He saw him standing next to Louie and his friends at the Hero Worship Bar. He saw Dirk in the center of a circle of admirers earlier that night; saw him posing for photographs. In every mental image Louie could dredge up of the golden superhero, he realized that there was one thing about Dirk that remained constant, no matter what the situation.

Dirk always had a hard-on.

Always.

"Oh, shit ... that's your weakness? Sex?" Louie asked in shock. "You can't have sex?"

"No. Not if I want to be able to do anything other than breathe," Dirk replied weakly. "Louie, you won't tell anybody about this, will you?" His voice was muffled against the carpet. "If my enemies ever found out that all they had to do to defeat me was to jerk me off, I'd be dead in the water – happy, but dead. God, my life fucking sucks. Do you know how painful it is to walk around with an erection all the time and never be able to do anything about it?"

A wide grin split Louie's face from ear to ear. Never, not once in a million years would Louie have ever thought that using Dirk's weakness against him would be so ... enjoyable. He slapped a hand lightly against Dirk's ass, making Dirk groan and tremble.

"Dirk, my friend ... we have to talk," Louie laughed. "I have a proposition for you, one that you're going to like ... a lot. It involves me, a tube of lube, a little work on my part, and a vacation for you once a week ... maybe more than once a week, if you're a good boy."

* * * * *

"Where's Dirk?" the Chief roared, his eyes scanning Headquarters as he burst out of his office. "I've got a runaway train, two buses of school kids dangling off a cliff, and a nuclear reactor that's about to reach meltdown! Where is he?"

"Uh, it's Saturday, Chief," The Cloaked Champion said, looking up from the newspaper he'd been reading. "It's his day off."

"It's his day to get off, you mean," Supersonic Man snickered quietly to Octoclops.

"Shit! Fine … Phil, you take the train. Larry, you get the school busses. Jack, you get the nuclear plant," the Chief grumbled, turning back to his office, "and for God's sake, smile for the cameras!"

Looking over Dirk's shoulder at the television screen, Louie grinned widely as he watched news clips of his friends saving the world. He turned back to the task at hand, namely thrusting himself deeply into searing kiln of Dirk's asshole. It's a dirty job, he thought happily, but somebody's got to do it.

Captain Chicken Hawk
By Mark Wildyr

The life of a superhero ain't all it's cracked up to be, let me tell you! Especially if you're the new guy on the block. Might not be so bad if I could just yell "Shazaam!" or "Cream Cheese" or something, but like that guy in the blue union suit and red briefs, I gotta find a phone booth or some nook or cranny when I go into action. And I don't like wearing my superhero gear under my street clothes ... it itches too much. So I have to change from the skin out! Superman's lucky he's in Gotham City. Me, I serve the Albuquerque metro area, which includes Rio Rancho, the "fastest-growing city in the US of A." Anyway, lumped together, there might be five hundred thousand souls and not one single telephone booth! All they have are these kiosk things, and there's precious little privacy there.

Once, as I changed into my working clothes ... I don't call it a costume ... to respond to a trouble call, some blue-haired old lady set up such a screech that I had to take off half-dressed. It gets chilly flying around with your ass hanging out. Tired of losing wallets to thieves while I'm performing heroic deeds, I now hang my street clothes in a tree or from a tall building somewhere.

There are other disadvantages, too! Like most guys, I like a big cock up my ass now and then ... or at least I believe I would. You think that's gonna happen? Not with these "buns of steel" I've got. I tried it a few times when I was a kid, but it was always a bust. The hunky jocks sweating over me usually end up cum-spraying my butt without ever penetrating the sphincter. The wet ends of their big dongs tickle the hell out of my rosebud, but no way are they going to penetrate it. Closest I've ever come is sticking a steel rod up my bunghole a few times and pretending it's some hot dude.

Of course, there was that time I rescued this cute transvestite from a couple of punks bent on beating her up. I reamed my ass with a lead pipe while that sweet thing went wild sucking my cock. Dyn-o-myte!

I'd like to meet some of my superhero peers sometime. Not that they're all that sexy. Superman looks pretty decent, but that jutting jaw is just too much. And have you ever examined his crotch? The thing's flat as a pancake. There's not even a worm under there! The Batman dude looks kinda good, and Robin might be a nice snack, but there are equally hunky fish to fry among the general population ... know what I mean?

The UNM campus out on East Central's got a few. It also used to have some restrooms with glory holes, but they're pretty much gone now. I remember once this dude was doing such a great job sucking my dick that I got carried away and left the impression of my body in the stall wall. Sometimes I forget my own strength.

Guess I should say something about my superhero name. As a kid just discovering I was different in every sense of the word, I found all the really neat names were taken. I was drawn to noble birds, you know, eagles and hawks and things like that. But I rejected "Eagle" because it calls to mind this big, bald-headed bird. Uncool. Definitely uncool. Since there's already a guy calling himself Hawk, I settled on "Falcon" and added the Captain part to give it some pizzazz.

My mom, the only soul in the universe who knows my secrets ... well, one of my secrets ... is totally ignorant of feathered raptors. So she copied a bird from a book and emblazoned it on the chest of a costume she whipped up. Wouldn't you know it? It wasn't a falcon; it was a hawk! Worse, some bird-watcher freak recognized it as a chicken hawk, and that was that. Little did anyone understand how appropriate the name was.

Mom is also the only person who knows where my powers come from, but she won't spill the beans, not even to me. She's mentioned my absent father exactly once to say he was "one of a kind." Makes me wonder if I was sired by a being from some far-off planet or something equally as weird. Guess it doesn't matter; I am who I am.

My real-life handle is Danny Daniels, and I make a decent living selling real estate. It keeps me out of the office and gives me a lot of freedom to pursue my real vocation as New Mexico's premier crime fighter. I used to just soar around over the town keeping an eagle ... uh, hawk-eye ... out for misbehaving miscreants, but that changed when I got this little electronic police scanner from Radio Shack that I turn down low and lug around in my brief case. My super hearing makes it audible to me, so now I can go about my business and still beat the cops to a crime scene. Let me tell you about the last time I answered its call.

* * * * *

A drive-by shooting on the west side pulled me and a nice young couple out of a walk-through of a luxury four-bedroom, two and a half bath. I sorta hated to let that one go. The good-looking husband seemed a bit uncertain about his masculinity, and I had already mentally calculated that if I could get him into the bathroom alone, he'd be hanging off my erection within two minutes while his pink tongue did all sorts of wonderful things. I'd already got kind of het-up a couple of times, once at the sight of his trim butt when he bent over to examine the fireplace and again as he stretched to open a cupboard over the range, which served to emphasize a very nice basket.

But I'm a dedicated guy. Besides, I already had his address and telephone number, so I quickly sneaked off to get properly attired and fly across town, drawing excited squeals from little kids walking home from school. I often wondered if they exclaimed something like, "Look! It's a bird! It's a plane! No! It's Captain Chicken Hawk!"

I was at the site of the shooting within minutes, and although an ambulance crew already tended the victim, no cops were on the scene. I immediately gained some altitude to see if I could spot the red '57 Impala mentioned on the police scanner. After a few looping circles over the immediate area, during which I almost got into a fight with a Channel Eleven news helicopter, I spotted a beautifully restored, low-slung pimpmobile, scuttling through the narrow streets of a semi-rural area about five miles to the southwest. The jazzy buggy looked downright suspicious to my highly developed intuition for crime fighting. Putting on a burst of speed, I landed on the road in front of the vehicle. The car screeched to a halt fifty yards away, and a lean, young face behind the windscreen stared at me in amazement. With my super vision, I saw the kid's expression harden with determination. Or desperation.

At any rate, the driver, who couldn't have been more than twenty, tromped on the accelerator, and the Chevy shot forward. At the last moment, I performed a neat somersault over the speeding car and grabbed the rear bumper, twisting the vehicle to one side. The Impala left the road and bumped across a rough, fallow field where it became mired in the sandy soil. The driver bailed and bolted without a moment's hesitation.

Once again, I took flight and landed in front of the youth, who came to such a sudden halt that he almost fell on his face. His look went from surprise to panic and warned me what was coming. He snatched a pistol from his belt and leveled it at me.

"Get out of my way, motherfucker!" he yelled in a baritone gone shrill with fear.

Oh, shit! Not that. I hate guns. Bullets can't hurt me, of course. Not injure me, but they sting like crazy, and I don't like that. So I obeyed him. Executing another graceful somersault, I landed behind the startled gunman. Before he knew what was up, I grabbed the black, thirty-eight revolver from his hand, seized him by the scruff of his neck, and took off. Fantastic! Not only had I nabbed the shooter, but I also had the weapon used in the drive-by. A slam dunk for the cops!

But the little fucker had other ideas. He immediately shrugged out of his muscle-shirt and landed in a heap back on the ground. Quick as can be, he scrambled to his feet and loped across the field, limping slightly. I hovered above him, holding his shirt and pistol in my hands and admiring the kid's spunk ... not to mention those wiry back muscles that rippled nicely as he ran. They gave me an instant hard-on, which played hell with my aerodynamics, I must tell you.

The kid was slender, almost thin, but his torso had decent definition. Brown skin wet with the sweat of his efforts and fear, glistened in the afternoon sun. I liked the way his waist narrowed as it disappeared beneath his belt. He was about to reach cover, so it was time to stop ogling and bring the kid to justice.

I swooped down and latched onto his belt, angling for some quick altitude to intimidate the kid. Didn't work. Before we were ten feet in the air, he slipped headfirst right out of his baggy, gangsta britches and fell back to earth with an audible grunt. If the guy was fetching before, now he was downright sexy. I blocked his way for the pure pleasure of watching his package roll beneath his white jockeys as he raced toward me. He came to another quick stop, panting and glaring at me wild-eyed. His chest heaved deeply ... erotically. Why would a handsome kid like this shoot another human being? The tattoos on both arms might have been clues. Perhaps it was a gang initiation.

"You gonna behave now?" I asked calmly, wondering if he could see the erection snaking down my leg. Tights don't conceal much, and they sure as shit don't have any maneuvering room. Despite the fact that it wasn't very "heroish," I carefully adjusted myself, bringing my pulsing member up against my flat, muscled belly. The kid noticed.

"Who ... who are you?" he demanded breathlessly.

I tore my gaze away from a study of his trim body, resisting the urge to use my X-ray vision to peek behind the cotton shorts. Oh, why the hell not? So I zapped in on a fat, uncircumcised cock resting atop a pair of brown nuts crammed into the briefs.

"Who do you think I am?" I asked calmly.

"You're that Captain … uh, Captain …"

"Hawk," I supplied helpfully.

"Chicken Hawk," he corrected contemptuously.

"If you want to get technical."

"Get outta my way, or I'll hurt you."

"If you've heard of me, kid, then you know that's not possible."

"Benno!"

"What?" I asked, momentarily disconcerted.

"My name's not kid. It's Benno."

"OK, Benno. You going peacefully now, or are you going to give me trouble."

"You've got a hard-on!"

"That's true."

"What kind of superhero gets a bone from looking at another guy?"

"Well, the guy's pretty much naked. And besides, I X-rayed your shorts and saw what's beneath them."

The kid cupped his crotch with his hands. "You a fucking fag or something? Whoever heard of a queer superhero?"

"I'm your worst nightmare," I replied with as much decorum as I could muster with a big, hard dick, distorting the silhouette of my tights. "I'm going to bring you before the bar of justice. Make a citizen's arrest."

The little punk laughed. "You talk like a comic book or something! Hell, you look like a comic book."

"That's the way superheroes talk," I sputtered indignantly. "Get used to it, kid. Now it's time to see you to the authorities to answer for shooting an innocent pedestrian."

"Innocent?" he snickered. "Fucker's a made gunman!"

"A rival gang, I presume," I responded, admiring the way he had recovered so quickly. His fine chest was no longer heaving. Sweat beaded on the expanse of smooth flesh between dark brown nipples.

My gangster gave a fetching, little-boy frown and shifted his stance, unconsciously twitching his cute bubble butt. "Fucker deserved it. Did I ice him?"

"Don't know. Saw the medics working over him when I came for you. At any rate, it's time to face the music."

Benno, if that was really his name, made a sudden lunge for me, but I merely clasped his forehead and held him at arm's length, letting let him flail away harmlessly. But he was a scrapper, my Benno, and in a moment he twisted himself free. Of course, he would have broken his fool neck if I hadn't released the pressure. He came at me again, slipping beneath my arms and grabbing me around the waist. We grappled, and to be honest, I let it go on for a few minutes for the pure joy of feeling those sweat-slick muscles struggle. Eventually, he wore himself out and sagged against me. I could almost hear the kid thinking; his body tensed as he made his decision.

"You ... you like me, don't you?" he asked hesitantly.

"You're nice to look at, but don't think I'd want you for my best buddy."

"But you want me! I can tell. I can still feel your boner." He ground his hips against me, rather desperately, I thought.

"Well, that doesn't help matters much."

"We ... we can make a deal. You can have me. Then you can just let me go. I got a big one ... and ... I really get it good when I cum! And you can have it."

"I've got the big one," I came back at him. "And you can have it."

He flinched. I suspected this wasn't going the way he'd planned. The kid swallowed hard. "Oh ... OK. I can jerk you off, I guess."

"No, thanks. I was thinking how pretty your mouth is."

"My mouth!" he almost screeched. "You want me to suck your cock?"

"I think the suggestion was yours."

As he reared back to look me directly in the eye, his handsome face turned weasel. The kid wasn't very good at hiding his thoughts. "Nobody has to know?" he asked tentatively.

"Just you and me."

"OK, I guess. Where?"

I pulled him to me and lifted off, heading for a nearby stand of trees. The fearless gang-banger was so terrified he wrapped his legs around one of mine, pushing that nice, full groin tight against me.

I found a suitable thicket and pushed Benno to his knees while I tugged down my form-fitting pants. The kid stalled, taking my thick cock in his hand and pumping a few times, but he wasn't going to get away with that ... even though it felt pretty damned good. It *had* been a long time. I put my hand behind his head and ordered him to take it.

He faltered a moment, and then his mouth reached for me, closing around my corona. He gagged immediately, came off, and tried again, doing better the second time. He set up an awkward, perfectly terrible herkey-jerky rhythm with little more than the tip of my cock in his mouth.

Then he did what I knew he had intended all along. His jaws clamped down viciously and his head jerked back and forth like a bulldog's. The fucker tried to bite off my dong! He couldn't of course, and while the pressure felt sorta good, his sharp teeth irritated me a little. I ignored him long enough for Benno to understand that it wasn't going to work and then clapped him sharply on both ears. He went about halfway limp, but I held him in place by the hair of his head as I threw my hungry cock to him. He was so dazed that he just slumped there groaning while I fucked his face.

Realizing that I still held his revolver in my hand, I came up with a brilliant idea. I reached behind me and carefully inserted the three-inch barrel up my anus. Wow! That felt good. Now I humped a warm, wet mouth and a cold steel barrel. Sha-fucking-zaam!

Like I said, it had been awhile, so I got there quickly. The kid had begun to cooperate by the time the old balls curled up tight against me, preparing to let loose a charge of hot semen. Benno pulled me to him just as things got serious. When my orgasm struck, he began to struggle, but I held his head in both hands as I pumped cum into him. I tend to cream a lot, and he was so sexy-looking that I might have got up a little extra for him. Then all of a sudden, there was a loud explosion, and I got an unexpected charge out of the thing.

Benno, the little turd, had discovered his pistol hanging out of my ass and pulled the trigger. I can honestly say I have never had an orgasm like that before. It stung a little bit and heated up the old insides, but frankly it hurt sorta good.

Mildly irritated, I pushed him over in the leaves and jerked off his shorts. It took two minutes of serious sucking, but old Benno finally responded and filled up my mouth with a column of hard, hot prick. He was groaning another tune when he finally exploded. The kid produced some pretty copious jism of his own.

Old Benno was shocked when I hauled him off to the law after he got dressed. Little prick shouldn't have tried to bite me ... not to mention shooting me up the ass. Aw, who am I kidding? I'd have turned him in regardless.

As I soared away from police headquarters with the hurrahs of admiring officers of the law ringing in my ears, I was secure in the knowledge that Captain Chicken Hawk had cleared the streets of Albuquerque of yet another desperate criminal.

Then I wondered how long it would take for me to poop a little lead pellet.

Captain Velvet
By Ryan Field

Once upon a time there was a shy young man who became unexpectedly famous through no fault of his own.

He was only twenty-two years old by then; a recent college graduate living in a rented Manhattan studio and working as a junior sales rep for a large advertising agency. Slim and athletic, with short, reddish brown hair parted perfectly on the right and a small, straight nose and strong, dimpled chin that suggested true Yankee origin, he wore preppy white shirts and casual khaki slacks and took pride in the fact he had always melted into the world quite naturally.

It hadn't occurred yet to Ross that he'd been blessed with a superhuman gift, a type of sensual magic, which could bring any man to his knees, begging for more.

The night he finally realized he was different from other men he was in bed with a guy he'd met at a downtown bar – a thirty-year-old Italian guy, Bruno-from-Brooklyn, with jet black hair and large muscles bulging all over the place. Though Bruno-from-Brooklyn pronounced his TH's as D's, and every sentence included the F word, Ross had liked the way he'd spread his legs wide and hiked up his jeans when he'd sat down at the barstool – a real butch type who smoked and drank beer straight from the bottle. The night they first met, Bruno wasted no time placing his great, strong palm roughly on the small of Ross's back to let all the other guys know Ross belonged to him and to make it clear that he would always be the aggressor. Though Ross wasn't feminine in any way, he clearly was the placid, fair-haired type most dark, forceful guys prefer.

But the lines were clearly drawn from the start. Bruno-from-Brooklyn had a wife, two children and a full time job as a New York firefighter. He was only looking for some fun and games and was only interested in quick sex with guys who had great asses. This was fine with Ross, still a virgin in many ways. He only wanted to gain some experience and wasn't about to transform Bruno. No use trying to change someone who was already ruined for life.

On the first night they went back to Ross's small studio apartment, Bruno practically tore Ross's clothes off and threw him down on the bed, where they kissed and hugged and groped each other like teenagers in the backseat of a car. Bruno was so desperate he never bothered to remove his clothes; just unzipped his tight jeans and let the big boy bounce out, pressing and rubbing it roughly into Ross's flat pelvis. Ross became the submissive, flat on his back, stark naked, while Bruno kept him pinned to the white sheets. They shared a perfect chemistry. Bruno sensed Ross needed to be guided, and Ross was aware that Bruno's ego needed to be boosted. But Bruno was in a hurry to get back to his wife, so the playing around only lasted about a half hour, ending with Ross on his knees, hands pressed firmly to the denim fabric still covering Bruno's strong thighs, quickly inhaling Bruno to a full, uninhibited climax. Though Bruno was extremely large and wide, man hungry Ross never once gagged and made it perfectly clear with innocent blue eyes he would finish the job without the need for tissues or paper towels.

"That was hot, baby," Bruno said, slapping Ross's bare buttocks on his way out the door, "I'll be back tomorrow night around nine for some more."

Ross, though quiet and reserved, had natural instincts when it came to men like Bruno, and he knew how to prepare for the following night.

When Bruno actually returned (you could never be sure they would), Ross greeted him at the door wearing a sheer, black mesh thong; they wasted no time with small talk. Within seconds, they were in bed, Bruno gazing into Ross's steel blue eyes, holding him tightly and then sticking hungry tongue down Ross's throat. Ross lifted smooth legs in the air and wrapped them around Bruno's wide body, reaching for a vile of lube on a round table beside the bed. He wanted to please his strong lover in any way possible.

"I've never done this before," he told Bruno, "You're the first."

Bruno stopped short, head cocked to the right, a wicked gleam in dark brown eyes, and said, "Then I'll be real gentle, baby."

And then Bruno quickly kicked off his black work boots, removed the black tee-shirt and tight black jeans. Still wearing white socks, he took the lube, lathered his hefty penis and slowly lifted Ross's legs in the air. By then Ross's eight-inch erection was pulsing for more, so he spread his legs wishbone style, arched his back and invited Bruno to have complete control.

"Are you ready for this?" Bruno asked.

Ross nodded. "You're so huge I'm a little scared, but I want you to be the first. You're the best looking man I've ever seen." It wasn't a total lie; Ross was a virgin, and he truly did think Bruno was hot looking, but he also wanted to stroke Bruno's ego a bit, too. So he embellished the part about Bruno being the best looking man he'd ever seen.

With a dynamic finger, Bruno lubed and stroked the soft, pink area and then slowly began to insert the head of his penis. A less urgent lover probably would have inserted a finger or two; just to relax and prepare the tender hole for something much grander – not Bruno. Ross remained silent, giving himself completely, trying hard to relax his muscles. It hurt at first, but only for a split second, and Ross suddenly realized what he'd been missing with men. A feeling of fullness; a missing piece of the puzzle had finally been found.

Bruno moaned. "Damn, what the ...? You got something fucking fantastic going on down there. I never felt anything like it before ... almost like a vacuum."

Ross then instinctively began to take control from the bottom. He suddenly realized he was moving certain muscles he wasn't aware he had. Muscles buried deeply within his body that could manipulate and tug and suck on long, hard objects. When he squeezed his anal sphincter, it was as though magic fingers came alive, jerking Bruno into a state of glorious, orgasmic frenzy – soft, gentle fingers that responded to hard thrusting motions. And Bruno, who was beyond ecstasy, soon learned the harder and faster he pumped and pounded Ross, the more those magic fingers jerked and tugged at his penis.

Bruno eventually nailed him into the cushioned headboard, shouting, "I'm gonna go off soon baby ... I can't take it much longer ... this is too fucking fantastic."

"Harder, Bruno! God you're so big! Don't hold anything back, man," Ross begged, realizing for the first time in his life that he was about to climax without touching himself. As he held Bruno's large biceps for support, he could feel the explosion building with each and every pound and thrust, his genitals tight and ready to explode.

There was a simultaneous bang that ended with exhausted, sweating Bruno falling on top of Ross's smooth body. Breathless, he kept moaning, "That was freaking unreal, man."

Speechless, and not totally understanding his gift, Ross just sighed, wishing he could go another round.

"Are you sure that was your first time, buddy?" Bruno asked, while he quickly dressed.

"Never did that before," Ross assured him, "But I liked it ... a lot."

"Baby, thanks for that; I needed it! You've got a magic box down there ... it's superhuman!" Bruno said, stuffing the big floppy thing back into his jeans and pulling up the zipper.

"Your welcome," said Ross, feeling as though he should be thanking Bruno, too.

Several moments later, he gave Ross a deep, hard kiss, running his large hand down Ross's backside, slipping his middle finger into the pink spot, and saying goodbye. But Bruno never returned, and Ross went back to the bars downtown to meet guys. For some reason, he always seemed to attract the same type, too – the Bruno-from-Brooklyn, blue collar, straight types who were always spitting on the ground; men who were so masculine and so rugged you'd never guess they were gay, tall and muscular, with broad shoulders and large donkey feet; guys who tossed footballs and were comfortable grabbing their crotches in public in a nonsexual way. They drank beer and farted, rarely bothering to remove their smelly socks during sex. These guys seemed to sense that Ross was what they wanted, as though he were giving off a subliminal scent that shouted, "Line up boys." But they treated him very well, almost like a delicate crystal goblet, especially after they learned the things he could to do them in bed.

One guy, an ex-minor league baseball player in his late thirties, actually bought Ross a Rolex. This baseball player, though not interested in a lasting relationship, would beg Ross to bend over, arch his back and spread his legs. And Ross never objected. The guy was really hot: Six feet tall, strong hairy legs and ten inches of wood that could often go three or four times in a single night. By that time, Ross had been with enough guys to understand his gift and work it to the limit, driving them nearly insane with pleasure. The baseball player swore Ross had another set of hands up his ass. Ross unexpectedly received the Rolex for being a good sport one night when the baseball player brought two of his drinking buddies over, and they all took turns nailing him into a brown suede ottoman.

Though Ross was always discreet and maintained a very low profile, a few of the guys he'd been with had boasted about his "sweet hole." One night, a film producer approached him in a bar and asked if he'd be interested in doing a film. He said he'd heard a rumor that Ross was "special." Ross was both taken aback and flattered, and he told the producer he'd have to think about it and get back. After all, he had good job he liked at the advertising agency, and if he were to appear in X-rated films, he might lose it. But the producer assured him he'd be able to remain anonymous and use a stage name; no one would ever know his true identity. The concept of the film was about a sexual superhero, a good looking young guy with sexual powers who could bring men to their knees. Though it would be reality in format, with the most straight-looking guys they could find, it would be total superhero fantasy, and Ross would be the star. The producer persisted, promising Ross a generous salary, and finally Ross agreed that as long as he could remain anonymous he'd give it a try.

The following weekend, he rented a car and drove to a warehouse in New Jersey where the film producer had a small studio – a long, gray box of a building with steel doors and concrete floors. A Saturday and the place was empty except for a small cluster of inexpensive cars parked near Warehouse 33C.

Ross went inside, where six good looking young guys were strutting around half dressed in football player uniforms. Guys who truly did look like football players, knocking around in the locker room; straight dudes talking about their girlfriends. The uniform colors were dark green and white, some guys in green helmets and white jock straps, others wearing shoulder pads and tight white pants with green side stripes. The set was quasi locker room, with a long steel bench and gunmetal gray lockers. The guys were talking as though getting ready for a game, joking around like clueless best buds; just passing the time. The producer noticed Ross standing alone and walked over, handing him a uniform.

"Here, put this on," he said, "It's your costume." Then he said to the other guys, "Captain Velvet's here, boys. We're gonna get started as soon as he's dressed."

Ross looked at the uniform and creased his brow. It was nothing more than a sheer, see-through, black cape, a black velvet hood that completely covered his face; and very strange black leather boots. They were coarse, black hyde, mid-calf, with hard chrome trim and six-inch Cuban style heels and chrome-tipped toes like pointed arrows. Very kinky and not something Ross would ever have imagined wearing in a lifetime. At least, as the producer had promised, his face and head would be totally covered with a velvet hood. So he stripped down to nothing behind the lockers and dressed for the part.

In full costume, as he entered the film set almost totally naked except for the sheer cape and high-heeled boots, the guys who were talking suddenly became silent. The crew, four middle-aged guys with sophisticated camera equipment, stared in amazement. That costume, with Ross's smooth round ass only clearly visible beneath the sheer black cape, took complete command of the room. Ross suddenly felt empowered, his smooth muscular legs gliding toward the steel bench, a soft clicking from the high-heeled boots keeping metered time. It occurred to him that a transformation had taken place; he just wasn't quite sure how to handle it.

The producer smiled. "Are we ready to make a movie, Captain Velvet?"

"Bring'em on," Ross shouted through the velvet hood, beginning to feel as though he could conquer the world, "and watch me knock these boys off like flies."

This was the first time Ross had taken on six guys at the same time – six strong, football player jocks, with powerful hands and strapping legs, pounding him from one end of the set to the other. At one point, four of them held him in mid-air while his head bounced and two took turns from behind. And though this was acting, it soon became perfectly clear these guys had also noticed something very different about Ross. The moment they entered the velvet hole, they began to moan and beg and plead for more of his superhuman magic. They weren't acting; they weren't good enough to act like that. Their moans were the real thing; their raised brows and wide eyes, marveling at what Ross's box could do, described the ecstasy perfectly.

The producer claimed he'd never shot a film so quickly. During one scene, with Ross bending over the locker room bench, holding a penis in each hand and two in his mouth, the two young actors who were behind taking turns panted and rolled their eyes while he drained them completely. There were no lost moments that day while shooting the film, no actors who couldn't "get it up." Ross knew how to please and conquer each one of them. And, best of all, during the climax scenes, as Ross brought each actor to a pinnacle so wild their toes curled, he somehow managed to reach his own explosion every time without touching his own penis. Six times in one film. The guys in the crew were actually applauding, not realizing that Ross-as-Captain-Velvet had such an appetite he could have knocked off two dozen more. As a curtain call, while the football players cheered and shouted, "Go baby," Ross let the camera guys bang him, too.

This film was the beginning of a very long career, which brought Ross a great deal of money and more fame than he could ever have imagined. Though he always remained anonymous, safely hidden behind the black velvet hood, he soon began to make personal appearances in gay nightclubs around the globe. He became one of those pop icons that ride the thin line between mainstream and porn, more often than not taking devoted male fans back to the dressing room to perform his magic for free, his legs over some hot looking guy's shoulders watching the ecstatic expression on the guy's face. For Ross, it wasn't about the money or fame; it was about making other men very happy; this became his mission in life. And though he had furtively become Captain Velvet, a cult legend, he never allowed this to define him and continued to work hard in the advertising agency until they finally promoted him to senior partner.

Gravitar
By Armand

"Do you ever wear shoes?" I asked jokingly while nodding toward her bare feet.

Terra gave me a look of perturbation and then leaned over the edge of the building to look down. We knew that there was a jewel heist going on in the building across the street, which is why we were hovering on a downtown rooftop at ten o'clock at night.

"Don't you want to wear some Jimmy Choos or Manolo Blahniks sometimes?" I continued.

"I'm a superhero, not Paris Hilton," she quipped. "Now are you going to help me down, or are you going to let those goons get away?"

"You just want me to touch you," I teased.

My power over gravity only worked on things I touched. If I had physical contact with something, or someone, I could alter the pull of gravity to either increase it, making the object uncharacteristically heavy or decrease it (making it almost weightless). The former was like wearing a suit made of lead while the latter was like being on the moon. As a teenager, I could levitate a car as long as I had my hand on its frame; as an adult, I can actually raise a jumbo jet off the ground. In fact, I can reverse the pull of gravity to actually propel my body, and the things I touch, away from the center of the earth.

My inherent limitation is that I can only raise or lower things in respect to the center of gravity. That means that I can't actually "fly" so much as "levitate." Once I levitated all the way into the clouds, but I was afraid I'd pass out and fall to the ground, like the boy who melted his wax wings, so I chickened out and descended quickly to safety. I am definitely not immortal, nor is Terra. I guess it's greedy, but I would love to be invulnerable, too.

"They're going to get away, Gravitar," she said as she stepped onto the ledge.

"You know we have to jump," I reminded her, as I stepped up next to her.

She threw herself off the building unexpectedly, catching me off guard. Luckily, I had a tight hold on her hand. It wasn't graceful or pretty, but I was levitating twelve stories above the pavement with Terra dangling like a Russian aerialist in my grip.

"Can't you get me down any faster?" she grumbled.

"Jeez, you're grumpy. PMS?"

"Now you sound like a straight guy. Just put me down, so we can end this. I got to get home; I've got a shirtless Hugh Jackman waiting in the DVD player."

She was speaking my language! I'd like to use my superpowers on Hugh one day.

Suddenly, I descended rapidly, as if gravity had resumed its natural pull, and we plummeted towards earth, the source of her power. I braked at the perfect distance, just when her toes touched the pavement. To her credit, even as we plunged towards the ground, she never flinched.

"What are you going to do?" I asked.

"The city commissioners are going to be pissed, but I'm gonna have to rip up another street."

Terra had amazing power, and sometimes I was jealous. Ultimately, I wouldn't trade my power for any other because it was mine, but I liked hers, too. The ground, more specifically dirt and clay, responded to her energy, so she could raise hills or even mountains with a simple willful command. Like me, however, she had to actually touch what she was manipulating, which is why she never wore shoes when she was in superhero mode. With her bare hands and bare feet she could command the earth within a large radius to bend to her will, and it was awesome to see.

Often, I found myself wondering about her shoe collection. I figure in her real life she was probably a shoe salesperson or a pedicurist because it would be so ironic. For someone who canvassed Plain City barefoot every night, her feet always looked well-groomed. Maybe she had a boyfriend with a foot fetish who massaged and oiled them nightly.

When she wanted to use extreme power, she crouched down so that her feet and hands all touched the earth.

This was one of those moments.

The thieves stormed out of the building and jumped into their car.

Terra had to find actual dirt to touch, and we were in the heart of downtown, the typical concrete jungle, so it was no easy feat. There was a swatch of grassy land between the sidewalk and the road, so she leapt like a ballerina, crouched down and began manipulating the dirt.

Generally, superheroes have a hard time holding back while another superhero is displaying superpowers, catching bad guys, or winning the adoration of onlookers, but this time I was willing to wait for Terra to do the dirty work – pun intended.

The robbers squealed the tires on their car as they pulled out onto the road and headed our way.

Then I heard the sharp crack of the pavement just before the broken asphalt rose up on a mountain of dirt right in front of the getaway vehicle. The momentum almost launched the car into the air, but instead it settled back on its rear bumper before sliding down onto its four tires again.

The robbers saw their chance for escape, so it was my turn to intervene. Before they could throw the car into reverse and speed away, I leapt onto the roof of their vehicle and levitated it nearly two hundred feet into the air.

"Shoot him," one of the thieves yelled.

"Yeah right," another protested. "If we kill him, then he drops us, and we all die."

"He's got a point," I gloated from my perch atop their car.

"Fucking superheroes."

"But that Terra's hot," one of them commented.

"Yeah. She's got a nice rack."

"Straight boys," I sighed.

I looked down and saw that Terra had formed a large earthen prison in the middle of the road. It was like looking into a volcano. Slowly, I began to lower the getaway car, with its irate passengers, into the pit.

"At least it wasn't Helios," one of them stated thankfully. "Now he's a badass."

Ahhh, Helios. He was the best, but I didn't want to hear about it from these hooligans, so I dropped the vehicle the last twenty feet. Hopefully, it gave them a little whiplash.

"Oops." I feigned concern as I bound off the vehicle and levitated in the air.

"Cops are on their way," Terra told me as I landed next to her.

"Bastards said that Helios is the real superpower in Plain City," I complained.

"Well, they're right."

"Sure he can harness the sun's power and shoot deadly rays, but that doesn't make him better than us."

As if taken aback, she leaned away from me and shot me a "who-the-hell-are-you-kidding" glance. "You on crack! The man is a god. He's got those cobalt eyes and that corn silk hair. And you've seen the way he fills out that yellow spandex costume."

"Yeah. That caboose could stop a clock," I swooned.

"And that black face mask and square jaw."

"All of those damn muscles. He must work out everyday."

"Too bad he's straight." She winked at me.

"Maybe he's not."

"In your dreams, Gravitar. He's too delicious not to be straight."

"How long have we been pining over him?"

"Too long."

She was right.

Sirens sounded in the distance, which was our cue that it was safe to leave.

"Come on. Let's go drool over some Aussie beefcake."

* * * * *

I had torn my costume again and needed to have it repaired. Luckily, ever since I'd saved the life of a seamstress, she'd sewn and repaired my hero costumes without question. My costume is green, for no other reason than I like the color. Like Helios, I wear a mask rather than a helmet for reasons that must have something to do with vanity. Terra, on the other hand, wears a tight-fitting costume of striated material that looks like layers of earth – chocolaty brown, tan, burnt red – and her mask has wings akin to a Val Kyrie headdress. Each of us has an emblem on our chest – must be a superhero thing. Mine is a white letter G inside a black circle; Terra's is a globe; and Helios's is naturally a sunburst. None of us wears a cape, but some days, I regret that decision. However, when I was conceiving my costume, I flew up into the atmosphere with a hoodie tied around my neck, and the damn thing nearly whipped me to death in the wind, so I immediately nixed the idea of a cape.

The three of us are all the superpower that Plain City can contain, though there is no shortage of corruption and crime. Sometimes I think that criminals flock here from the entire east coast just to test our powers.

Terra surfaced the year after I donned my costume and became a justice fighter. Helios showed up two years later, looking better and showing his flashy powers. None of us knew the other's true identity, but I definitely wanted to make my super-fantasies come true with Helios.

Terra and I had fought side-by-side on several occasions. She knew that I was gay from the first time we met, making me think she was a fag hag in real life – though I'd never say that to her – and she constantly ribbed me about being a gay superhero.

On separate occasions, Terra and I both had fought beside Helios, but the three of us had never fought together. Whenever he shows up at a scene, it is a double-edged sword. It is a treat for my eyes and my libido, but he is so hot that he distracts me from the crisis at hand. And it is hard to hide one's excitement in spandex. I could get killed watching his ass instead of the bad guys.

Helios was like the big man on campus or the all-American athlete, and his charm knew no limits. He was so sexy and flirtatious that he always eclipsed me. Reporters loved him, kids adored him, and the freaking PTA worshipped him. The local deli even had a sandwich named after him! If he wasn't so damn hot, I might have resented the guy. But I had to admit that he was just a little ray of sunshine in a cold, inhospitable world.

One May afternoon, the three of us got our chance to fight together.

I was dancing through the apartment in my underwear – don't ask – when I saw the news flash on the TV. It was a hostage situation at an elementary school. Some buffoons had tried to kidnap the local billionaire's son, and the kid foiled their plan when he figure out something was wrong, kicked one of them in the shin, and ran away screaming like a banshee. Good for him. Unfortunately, the would-be crooks panicked when they spotted the police and took eight children hostage onto the roof to await a helicopter. Yeah, dumb asses!

I arrived at the scene with a rip in my costume just below the belt, so the band of my jockstrap was visible. Of course, Helios had to be on the scene when I arrived. For a moment, I debated which was more important – my dignity or the kids being held hostage. Damn, a good conscience can be hell!

"So we going to do it?" Helios asked in that trademark husky voice.

Then he had to do it; he looked down at the tear in my costume.

"Going to do what?" I asked and then recovered from my embarrassment long enough to realize that he was referring to saving the kids and capturing the bad guys. Nice to know that my mind could be in the gutter even while a catastrophe was ensuing. Finally, I responded, "Let's do it."

"You boys might need a woman's touch," a familiar voice called from behind. "After all, there are children involved."

Then she had to do it, too: She glanced down at the tear and gave me a questioning look.

"I was crime fighting," I stated huffily.

"Jeez, Gravitar, there are kids around you know." Her sarcasm could be caustic.

Helios chuckled, adding salt to my wound.

"Our first threesome," Helios commented excitedly, and Terra and I blushed at the insinuation. "So who's got a plan?"

The umbrage of being ridiculed for my wardrobe malfunction made me slow to respond, so Terra beat me to the punch. "I could send firmament up the sides of the building and onto the roof, but I can't see the kids to bury them in safety bubbles."

"Why can't one of us fly?" Helios asked.

"I levitate," I bragged, but it sounded lame, and I wanted to eat my words.

"That's right. So you can fly me over there?"

"I can't move laterally like that. I can raise you by reversing the pull of gravity on your body."

"How can we get close to the building, so you can do that without those morons seeing us and picking us off with their rifles? And why isn't one of us invulnerable?" The blond hunk was gorgeous, but he seemed to have a bit of superpower envy. "And none of us has invisibility."

Terra cast a knowing glance at me. We didn't care if he wasn't the sharpest tack in the shed; we both wanted to jump his bones.

"Underground," Terra announced. "Boys, time we act like moles."

"Niiiice," Helios drew out the word like a surfer might. "Then Gravitus can levitate me to the roof where I can put on a show."

He doesn't even know my name! *It's Gravitar, not Gravitus.* Will the fun never stop! I wanted to go home.

"You can levitate me to the roof, can't you? I'm not too heavy?"

"Sure," I snipped. What was the point of telling him I could lift a jumbo jet when he doesn't even know my name? "But I have to be touching something to affect the pull of gravity on it."

He shrugged and said, "Cool. You can touch me. After all, I might like it." Then he clapped me on the shoulder. "Let's do this," he said to Terra.

I got the pleasant task of informing the police of our plan. Luckily, Plain City's finest loved having the three of us on the job with them, so they volunteered to distract the kidnappers by talking to them over megaphones, while we approached from the rear of the building.

The closest place to the school where we could secretly descend underground was in a copse of trees in the distance, so we rushed there. The cool air tickled my skin through the hole in my costume, reminding me of my feelings of inadequacy. I'm a damn superhero; I shouldn't feel insufficient. But the hunk in yellow spandex who could harness the power of the sun didn't make it easy to feel special in this town.

"How are we going to know when we're there?" I asked suspiciously.

"Good question," Terra said. "I can take us underground, but I can't tell what direction we're going and how far we've gone."

"Look, it's a straight shot," Helios insisted. "It's about fifty yards. We're supers; we can figure it out."

We both doubted his certainty, but his confidence was very sexy. I began to think that he was the only one of us that acted like a superhero.

Terra planted her hands next to her beautiful feet, and the earth in front of us began to separate as if an invisible bulldozer was excavating it. The earthworms and beetles shifted along with the dirt, and exposed roots from trees dangled in the opening. Any rock that was unearthed fell to the bottom, because Terra could not control rocks at all. For some reason, I always fantasized that she had a secret twin brother who could control stones. Of course, in these fantasies, he was always hot and gay, too.

"Damn, she's good," Helios said to me.

That bitch was showing me up! Just wait till I got the chance to wow him with my mighty powers.

"Ladies first," she said as she stepped down and entered the tunnel she had formed in the ground.

With every step, the dirt in front of us separated, forming a chasm just wide enough and tall enough to allow us easy passage. She simply dragged her hands along the sides of the earthen tunnel and planted her feet firmly on the ground, and the dirt responded like metal shavings moving towards a magnet. Soon we were far enough that we were losing the light from the entrance.

"A little sunlight to guide us," Helios said as he extended his hand and created a glowing orb of light.

I wondered if above ground, the criminals could see a trail of raised earth like in a cartoon, but I didn't want to know.

"Damn it," she exclaimed. "A boulder."

"Can't you move it?" he asked.

"I can move the earth around it but not the rock. I'll see if I can get us around it."

"I could shatter it with my sunbeam, but it would make a mess, besides a lot of noise."

"We don't have much time," I announced. "Just let me raise it out of our way."

I touched the behemoth and lifted it up only enough to allow us to crawl underneath. Hopefully, the bad guys didn't see the ground buckling or the rock breaking through the surface.

After a few more minutes, Helios yelled, "Stop. I think we've gone the right distance."

"If I open the tunnel over our heads and we get shot, I'll be more than a little pissed," Terra insisted.

"Relax. We got this."

"Ready?" she asked.

"Let's do it."

Terra opened a ramp of earth before us. Wanting to prove my bravery, I started my ascent, but I'd hesitated a hair too long, and Helios beat me to the front.

We ascended no more than three feet from the elementary school. The bastards wouldn't see us unless they were leaning over the edge of the building looking down, which thankfully they weren't.

"OK, you're up Gravity Man," he whispered.

It's Gravitar you blond airhead!

"Raise you up to the roof?" I asked without the slightest hint of enmity for him butchering of my name. "And then what? There're five of them."

"Close your eyes because it's going to get a little bright. Anyone with their eyes open will have some problem seeing for a few hours."

"What if they begin shooting?"

"They'll aim at us, not the kids."

Oh great! Just what I wanted to hear.

"Don't' let them hit you." He smiled as if he was in a toothpaste commercial. I had the strongest desire to grab him and kiss him on the lips, but then he might blast me with his sunbeam, which could hurt.

"It might get a little noisy," Terra whispered. "I'll raise a ramp up the side of the building, so tell the kids to jump."

"That's a lot of earth to move to reach the roof." Questioning her power, he raised his brows.

"You don't think I can handle it, Helios? I'm a whole lot of woman with a whole lot of power. They may need to do a little landscaping at the school after I'm done."

This whose-is-the-biggest banter was getting me frustrated, and the double entendres were not helping.

"How does this work?" Helios asked me. "You've got to touch me in a special place?"

The bastard was teasing me in the middle of a crisis! I'd touch him in a special place alright, and he'd like it.

"Yeah. I have to grab your dick."

"Ooh. Go for it."

I had no smart-alecky comeback. For a moment, I considered actually grabbing his dick, but I just responded by saying, "Turn around."

"Good. I like that, too." He turned and then purred, "Be gentle, daddy."

I grabbed him roughly and just for spite – or a cheap thrill – I thrust my crotch into his rock hard ass.

He looked back over her shoulder and cooed, "If you don't drop me, I'll make out with you later."

Terra's eyes were wide, and so was my smile as I lifted us slowly off the ground. Once we passed the first floor, I picked up speed and shot us over the edge of the roof in a flash.

Just in time, I remembered to close my eyes and the blast of light even burned through my eyelids. Voices began yelling in front of me, and a rumbling like an earthquake sounded behind me.

Then I felt Helios struggle free from my clutch. He dropped onto the rooftop, rushing into the center of things, and I stepped onto the ledge and joined him.

"Kids, it's Gravitar," I called. "Follow my voice. I'll help you."

Helios shot a concentrated beam of white light from his palms and knocked down two men in rapid succession.

Two goons who were located near me raised their rifles to shoot, so I jumped indelicately and touched them both at one time. Rather than loosen the gravitation pull on their bodies, I ramped it up tenfold and dropped them like dumbbells at the gym. They hit the rooftop so hard that the gravel imbedded into their skin. One of them fell on his firearm, which would surely leave a permanent indentation.

Helios began herding the kids, as he manically searched for the fifth gunman.

"Follow my voice, kids," I yelled, and they obeyed.

Then I dragged the prostrate bodies roughly to the edge and stood atop them as I helped the first kid off the roof. Terra had created a crater of earth, much like a giant hand, and she rose up from the center of it and caught the child.

"There's one more," Helios yelled. "Where is he?"

"Give me the kids," Terra commanded.

Helios was worried about the last gunman, and Terra just wanted to save the kids. I was trying to do both.

I picked up the last kid and tossed him just as a gun swung out from behind a vent.

As long as I've been at this superhero thing, I still marvel at how time begins to move in slow motion during intense moments like this one.

I heard myself yell and saw Terra catch the child and turn to protect him. She wasn't invulnerable, so a gunshot would just as likely kill her as any of us, but she acted selflessly. OK, so now I wasn't so mad at her for making me look bad earlier.

Helios threw up his hand as I rushed toward the assailant. A blast of light stopped me in my tracks, knocking me off my feet.

Then there was silence.

"Guess they'll need to replace that vent," Helios commented matter-of-factly.

I looked back, and there were no signs of Terra. She had already carried the children to the ground on a wave of … well, ground, and left Helios and me to fend for ourselves.

"Why do you look so concerned?" the sunny superhero inquired. "Did you think I might have been shot, and you wouldn't get to make out with me?"

The two gunmen I had abandoned began to rise from the rooftop, gravel and tar still stuck to their faces.

"I wouldn't do anything rash boys," Helios said as he held out his glowing palms. "After all, I've got a date with Gravitar here tonight, and I don't want to miss it."

So he does know my name!

Helios smiled at me and winked.

"And we've really got to get that costume repaired," he added.

I looked down and saw that the tear had gotten much bigger and more of my jockstrap was showing. All I could do was smile. I was going on a date with Helios, so I really didn't care.

* * * * *

An hour later, we found ourselves on the highest rooftop in Plain City. (After all, we couldn't go to his place or mine because we couldn't reveal our secret identities. And Helios and I renting a hotel room would cause an unfortunate stir in the media.)

No sooner had we landed on the rooftop than he grabbed the back of my head and planted a deep, animalistic kiss on my lips, and his tongue tasted divine. This was the moment I had dreamt of thousands of times.

Then he reached into the hole in my uniform and slid his hand into my jockstrap, grabbing my dick. I reached around him and squeezed his round, firm buns.

"Yeah," he said. "I've wanted to do this since the first time I saw your picture in the newspaper. That day you had saved a woman and her child from drowning, and I said, 'One day I'm going to make love to that man.'"

"I fantasized about this, too, but Terra convinced me that you're straight."

"Oh, I go both ways, but I love a hot dick, especially up my ass."

My eyes grew wide. Could it be that I was actually going to get to fuck this stud?

Then he dropped to his knees and began sucking my cock. I heard the fabric of my costume rip further, but I didn't care. Guess my grateful seamstress would just have to make me a new one. I rubbed his blond locks and caressed his ears while he blew me.

It is amazing how fast the two of us stripped our costumes off, and I nearly fainted when I saw his body. Barrel chest with a light dusting of blond hair, delicious round pink nipples, trimmed bush and thick cock, and two glorious balls hanging delicately below his erect penis.

It was my turn to drop to my knees, and I serviced his cock as if I were being graded. He moaned, and I gagged as I deep throated his thick member. Nothing could stop me from sucking that beautiful tool, except the words, "Will you lick my ass?"

OK, I jumped at that chance, and I spun him roughly and tongued his deep crack as if I were digging for gold. He had just a few blond hairs around his perfect pink pucker, which was the prize between two muscular pillows of flesh. Man, that superhero could moan! I knew that he was enjoying himself, so I popped a wet finger inside his tight hole, and he begged for more.

I couldn't stand it anymore, so I stood and rubbed my cock up and down his crack. He pulled a condom and a packet of lube from his boot, so I slipped on the rubber and greased up, then poked my dick at his tight hole. When I felt my organ sliding into the stud's ass, a quiver went through my entire body. I pulled him roughly backwards and felt my entire cock bury inside him.

"Oh yeah, Gravitar. Give me that big dick."

"You want it, Helios?"

"Yeah. Fuck me, superhero."

"Take it, superhero."

So I pounded the shit out of his muscular ass. Then I flipped him on his back and slid back inside his hungry hole in one deep thrust. He was stroking his rock-hard cock as I began to levitate us into the air, which allowed me to slide his whole body up and down on my penis.

"Fuck me harder, Gravitar."

"Like this!" I exclaimed as I pounded my cock into his ass.

Suddenly, my sun-powered friend began to glow yellow. I felt warm energy flowing out of his hands and into my body and light surrounded us in a bubble as we levitated six feet off the rooftop.

He started to cry out as cum shot from his cock into the air and landed across his chest and abdomen. I held him with one hand, so I didn't lose control of his body, and then ripped off the condom and shot on his cock and balls. Then I leaned forward and kissed him deeply. Before returning us to the rooftop, I licked his cum from his chest and abdomen.

"That was hot superhero sex," he said.

"Amazing," I responded through labored breath.

"You know how to fuck. Hope you want to do it again."

"Anytime."

"So can I see you without your mask?" Helios asked.

It was so unexpected that I couldn't formulate a response.

"I want you to know who I am," he said as he reached for his mask.

He tugged at it momentarily and then his face was revealed, and I let out a gasp.

Storm Boy (A Comic Strip)
By Henry Kujawa

Follow the adventures of Stormboy & Jay in the upcoming STORMBOY #2: IS THAT YOU?

Hummingbird (or Confessions of a Smitten Superhero Sidekick)
By Sedonia Guillone

The press, his fans, the unappreciative dicks down at the Agency, and the asshole criminals he vanquishes night and day, call Liam "The Hummingbird." I guess I can't blame them for having given him such a superficial title. They only know him from the outside, watching his magnificent, muscular body fly through the air at top speeds, hovering, moving up and down, backwards and forwards, snatching criminals from helicopters and airplanes as they make their getaways, saving screaming women and children from burning buildings and such.

Yeah, I know they can imagine the valiant heart beating in that broad chest dusted with swirls of raven dark hair, but they don't know him all the way through, like I do. (And I wouldn't want them to. I have a terrible jealous streak.)

No one asks me anyway, however, because I'm only the sidekick. Sidekicks (a degrading expression for me considering that my hands and feet are registered with the Agency as deadly weapons and spend great deals of time covering The Hummingbird's ass – OK, pun not intended) are never as important as the main superhero. Look what happened to Bruce Lee as Kato. Talk about getting shafted in the bad way!

To me, Liam Conner is an absolute wonder. Not because he can fly and because he's drop-dead fine, but because of who he is. Of course, that's the whole point of my writing all this down (and yes, I will give the delicious details even though I'm probably the only one who will ever read this memoir). Uh oh. Sounds like he might be waking up.

Looks over shoulder to where Liam's still sleeping in bed. Sigh of relief that eyes are closed, mind is oblivious to what lover/sidekick is doing behind his back.

Liam would be pissed if he thought I was writing about him and not keeping my daily log of our exploits for the Agency. Uh oh, the sheet has slipped down, giving me a full view of his perfect hard ass.

Stirrings of a raging hard-on in sidekick.

If Liam weren't so exhausted from saving the world, I'd slip right back in with him and ...

Sighs as forces self back to writing.

I guess you could say my complete body/soul devotion to him is because I burn for him through and through. Who wouldn't after eight years of working together (and well ... relaxing, too ... night and day)? And after what he did for me. But I'm getting ahead of myself. In order to convey the fullness of my feelings for him, I'll have to start at the beginning of our ... ahem ... association.

It was actually Hummingbird who saved my ass first.

I don't know what the hell Liam was doing in Hong Kong, but to my great fortune, he was there at the exact moment some thugs I had the grievous misjudgment to borrow money from tracked me down at my father's grocery store to collect. If I'd had the fighting know how then that I have now, (at the time I only bore a strong resemblance to Bruce Lee without his martial arts skills, whereas today I can immodestly brag of both), I would have been able to whirl, kick and punch my way out of the situation and save my father's lifelong toil and only meal ticket from being torched. However ...

The conversation went something like this:

Thug 1: "You owe Ling, and he wants it tonight, *si fut jai*." (That's Cantonese for homosexual. I don't know how he knew.)

Me: "*Diu lay.* (That's Cantonese for fuck you. I was an arrogant kid at nineteen.) Ling will get his money when I have it."

Thug 1 (pulling gun from hidden holster in belt): "You're going to be sorry you just said that, *si tao*." (That's Cantonese for shit head.) Nods to Thugs 2 and 3 who grab me and drag me out the door of my father's pathetic little store while Thug 1 picks up a large canister of cooking oil off shelf, spills it everywhere and lights it.

Out in the street, Thugs 2 and 3 whaled on me, punching and kicking, doing everything to get their point across that Ling was going to get his money tonight. All I could do was hold my gut, my body rolled up into a ball on the pavement, while in the background, my father's whole life went up in flames.

Suddenly, all fists and boot kicks receded, and I could hear Thugs 1 through 3 all grunting as the thud of fists on flesh reverberated all around me.

I blinked and looked up in time to see one of the thugs fly smack into a parked car and crumple to the ground, moaning and clutching himself as I was. Meanwhile, the roar of flames thundered in my ears, signaling the end of my parents' livelihood and probably my being disowned by both mother and father.

I closed my eyes, giving in to my abject misery. Suddenly, a pair of hands slid under my body, lifting me off the pavement like I was a rag doll. This was no easy feat, considering that even though I'm no giant at five foot nine, I still boasted a hard set of muscles, which were considerably weighty.

Whoever was holding me, however, was twice my musculature and obviously over six feet tall, for as he lifted me, the ground seemed to recede quite far.

Then it got even farther. We were floating, lifting off the ground, cutting through the humid summer air. My stomach lurched, and my instinct was to grab something. However, there was nothing to hold onto but the hardness of male muscle covered, it felt like, by the thinnest layer of clothing.

"Don't worry. I've got you," the low voice thrummed in my ear, and my beaten body immediately relaxed, in spite of the fact that the colorful Hong Kong skyline was passing by, literally, a few feet from my head, and I wasn't in an airplane or anything.

The night wind caressed my face and revived me. Not even the beating I'd gotten stood up to this night ride.

I don't know how long we coasted until this guy ... whoever he was (my heart and body already pulsing with desire) ... sailed over the top of a building and landed. Absently, I registered the large red neon sign of some fancy hotel of which we were on the roof, while my rescuer gently set me onto my feet, one large hand splayed warm and strong on my back, steadying me.

"Are you all right?" A sexy accent tinged his words, one I know now to be Irish, since Liam's from Dublin originally.

I blinked several times, gripping his arm (fingertips registering the hard muscles flexing underneath them) before I nodded, and he moved away, giving me space to catch my breath. Another few moments passed before I could keep my eyes open and look at my rescuer's face.

When I finally did, though, I was a fucking goner. Even in the shadowy light, I could see the large blue eyes, dark hair, (almost as black and smooth as mine but shorter, more like he was in the military or something), incredibly high cheekbones and soft lips made to do the most sinful things ...

I started to check the rest of him out, but got suddenly lightheaded, I guess, from the beating and the distress of knowing I'd just destroyed my father's life. I wobbled, unable to stop myself from heading toward the ground.

His arms shot out, catching me just as I fell. "I knew I shouldn't have let go of you," I heard him mumble, the sound full of self-blame.

Don't be so hard on yourself. I'm the fuck-up here, I wanted to say, my semi-conscious state made speech impossible.

I must have blacked out, for when I opened my eyes, I found myself on a bed, my shirt open and Mr. Gorgeous wiping my bare chest with a warm washcloth. He swiped the cloth gently across my pecs, the material causing sparks of delicious heat in my nipples. Damn, he had the sexiest touch, not that my experience at the time had been so vast to know the difference. I was actually pretty shy for all my arrogance and braggadocio.

Those thugs must have given my brain pan quite a working over because it took me that long to realize who this guy was. When the knowledge did hit me, however, I started shaking. What would he ... I mean The Hummingbird ... do to me when he realized he'd just wasted his superhero powers on a *si futt lou* (That's Cantonese for asshole.) like me?

His velvety, sexy lips curled into a sudden grin as he wiped the cloth down my stomach and back up again. "I'm not going to hurt you, you know."

I stared at him, my cheeks growing hot. I went to sit up, but pain shot through my shoulder.

"Easy now," he crooned, two fingertips on my chest easing me back against the pillows.

To make matters worse, I was getting a hard-on and was unable to hide the way my rising cock tented the front of my jeans. I hung my head against the humiliation.

"What's your name?"

I sighed, causing a slice of pain in my ribcage. Those goddamn thugs! Oh well, I deserved it. "Kit," I mumbled.

"Nice to meet you, Kit. I'm Liam."

My gaze shot up. His blue-eyed gaze met mine.

A lump formed in my throat. I'd never seen such a look before. It warmed me to my toes and made me want to cry. I didn't know then why, but I do now. The way he looked at me made me feel wanted, special, even in that first moment.

*Swipes at eyes with fingertips because deep down he's a sentimental slob. *

"You're ...you're ..."

"The Hummingbird." His expression turned a bit mournful, as if he didn't exactly enjoy being a superhero. I remember even thinking in that moment that he actually looked ... lonely.

"But ... you told me your real name."

He chuckled, but just as quickly his grin faded. "That real name stuff is only from the movies and comics. Me mum knows me real name and any bloke who grew up with me in Dublin knows it as well. One picture in the paper, and I've no hope of a cover."

My heart lurched. I'd certainly seen his picture in plenty of Hong Kong papers and on the Internet. If I had a dollar for every time I'd jacked off over his photograph, I wouldn't have had to borrow money from Ling.

Liam seemed to be hovering quite close to me, and I prayed he didn't see the raging woody I had for him, though I'm certain he did.

He rinsed the cloth out in a bowl, wrung it and pressed it to my forehead. His touch sent another thrill of heat through my already aching cock. "Those are some bruises they gave you."

I sighed again. "I ... thank you for ... helping me out." I closed my eyes against my shame. "But I thought you only save good guys."

"You mean you're not a good guy?"

I opened my eyes to see him smiling at me. This time, I got a better look at him. He was just as magnificent in the light, and I could see the broad muscles of his chest and shoulders pushing against that thin beige material he wore. I guess that kind of clothing makes his job easier.

I don't know what possessed me, but I ended up spilling my whole story beginning with my father's illness, the debt I incurred by borrowing the money from Ling for the doctor's bills, and giving his thugs the attitude that got my father's store burned and my ass kicked. When I'd finished, I fell silent, certain he would see me in the same ugly light I saw myself.

"You want to know how I happened to be nearby when they came for you?"

His soft question made me look up, my heart racing. I nodded, speechless.

A shy look stole into his blue eyes. "I saw you earlier today, carrying crates into that store."

The nerve endings of my entire body tingled. He'd watched me unpack a shipment of vegetables from a farm outside Hong Kong?

He chuckled, looking a bit shy. "Aye. Now you know the truth, right? I can't tell you my reasons for being in Hong Kong in the first place (he has since filled me in on the details of his assistance to the Hong Kong police), but when I saw you, I knew I had to take my chances for a second look."

At first I could only stare at him. Then ... I don't know what came over me ... I've never been ... aggressive. I launched myself at him, my injuries completely forgotten and covered his mouth with mine. My hands went to his shoulders, those broad, hard shoulders, the heat of his skin shimmering right through the thin clothing.

I almost died right then and there. His lips tasted so damn good, musky and delicious with a touch of something like mint.

He pulled back, his expression sad, belying the simmering in his eyes. "You don't have to repay me like this, you know."

Instant humiliation. Rejection made my face burn as hot as my father's store. I slumped back against the pillows, caught in a sudden fit of shivering. My teeth chattered mercilessly, and I felt as if I were naked in freezing weather.

"Oh bloody hell," he muttered. "What a clod I am." The next thing I knew, he was shedding that skintight getup he was wearing, peeling it off like the top layer of an onion.

I almost forgot my misery, my body shivering on its own, my stare glued to his body. As I mentioned earlier, swirls of silky dark hair covered his broad chest. A narrow swath of that hair streamed down his hard stomach, tapering into a dark trail down the center. His nipples the dark reddish brown of burnt cinnamon, made my mouth water to lick them.

I nearly gasped when he peeled off the bottom of his Hummingbird outfit. The first part of him I saw (and which is still one of my favorites) was his ass. Two pale perfectly hard globes made my hands itch to palm them and to slip my fingertips into the crevice between them.

His foot caught on the bottom as he slipped them down, and he hopped around, struggling for balance, giving me a clear view of the mouthwatering package between his legs. His balls were full and heavy, like two perfectly ripe plums in a sack. His powerful thighs, dusted with dark hair, flexed as he hopped about, struggling with his outfit.

I might have laughed at his struggle, but there was something achingly ... human ... about seeing the superhero grapple with something as simple as pulling off his clothes.

He finally succeeded in getting them off and turned around, approaching the bed. His blue eyes reflected a sheepish look. "I didn't mean to make you feel rejected," he murmured. "It certainly wasn't my intent."

I couldn't answer, only stare, my gaze sliding past the smooth hair in the furrow of his stomach muscles to his hard cock, the stretched skin reddish purple over the hard muscle.

"Let's get you undressed."

My blood turned icy hot in my veins, my heart pumping like mad. I was about to be completely naked with The Hummingbird. Maybe those thugs had actually beaten me to death, and this was heaven?

Large gentle hands drew my body forward, slipping my shirt off my arms. Then he reached down and pulled the covers back, a shy grin curving his lips. "Now for the rest of it."

I pulled off my socks, my hands trembling and then undid my jeans. I worked them down to my thighs, letting Liam slip them down my legs. There was absolutely no denying my hard-on now, my cock poking my underwear so hard it looked as if it might tear right through the cotton.

A tense but simmering silence passed between us. I couldn't break it because I was speechless.

He grinned. "Um, well, you can leave your skivvies on, but ... we may have an easier time of it without them."

Staring at him, my mind going numb now, I slid my briefs past my ass and hips, letting him pull them the rest of the way off. And then ... I was as naked as he was.

To my shame, I started shivering again, my teeth chattering with a violent clacking sound.

"This is the only way I know of to warm you properly." He slid in next to me, covering us both with the blanket. The next thing I knew, his broad, hard body was flush to mine, pressed against me, half covering me. Warmth radiated from his skin, the paleness of which contrasted beautifully with the golden hue of mine.

Without thinking, I pushed up against him, fitting perfectly to him in spite of the difference in our height and size. His soft chest hair tickled my pecs, causing my nipples to tingle in the same way they had when he'd rubbed me with the washcloth.

I still couldn't speak, but my hand knew what to do, my arm curving around him, my hand palming his back. His cock nudged my thigh, and it was all I could do not to roll onto my back and beg him to fuck me. I dared to let my hand slip lower, my fingertips tracing the ridges of muscles along his spine, venturing toward the smoother area of his ass.

His breathing, raged in my ear, pulsed heavily. "Kit, forgive me, please. I ..."

I couldn't let him go on apologizing when he'd saved my life and was giving me the fantasy of a lifetime. I shut him up with my lips over his. There was his delicious flavor again, musk and mint, and this small taste of him made me wild for more.

I pushed his lips apart with my tongue, invading his mouth hungrily. He groaned softly, the sound vibrating between our mouths. His hands slipped into my hair, which I was now very glad I kept on the long and shaggy side. I'd always taken great pride in my hair, using it to my best Bruce Lee look-alike advantage.

Feeling the effect I was having on him only spurred me on. His fingertips raked through my hair, the gentle pressure of his hands pulling our mouths tighter together. His tongue dueled wildly with mine, hot and moist, and I couldn't help feeling that the kiss was connecting us deeply.

I surged up over him, my injuries forgotten, pressuring him onto his back. I slipped one hand from around his back, now satisfying every fantasy I had about touching his incredible body. I raked my fingers through his chest hair, palming those broad muscles, my thumbs brushing his nipples into tight buds.

He moaned generously, the sound making me feel like I was a god of love ... or something equally as glorious ... and I resolved to bring him to the greatest heights I could.

I pulled away from his lips, my desire to taste the rest of him the only thing giving me the strength, and trail kisses down the side of his throat, stopping at the little hollow to swivel the tip of my tongue around. He seemed to love that and pressed his large hands hard into my back, silently urging me on.

I licked and suckled his collarbone, loving the salty warm taste of his skin and the appreciative way his fingers curled into my hair. Kissing my way to each nipple, I suckled long and hard on each one, the musky flavor rolling sweetly over my tongue.

I heard him panting freely now, subtly pushing my head to go lower. I was more than happy to do whatever he wanted and continued my trail of kisses down his stomach, following the scrumptious dark trail of hair.

Stopping at his navel, I pushed the tip of my tongue into it, wiggling it around the delicious hole until Liam was moaning my name. I'd never heard a sweeter sound in my life and knew even in my fevered haze that I was crazy in love with him and never wanted to leave his side.

Lingering there, I let my hand wander down to his cock, my fingers dragging through the soft hair around the base. His *lok chat* was thick and hard and twitched against my hand as I closed my fingers around it.

Just feeling the silky skin over that hard shaft made me have to taste it. Damn, I couldn't even bring myself to tease him, hungry as I was to have his cock in my mouth.

"Kit."

The way he said my name was more a request for my attention than a moan of pleasure. I looked up at him.

His blue eyes had darkened, his lids heavy. "I just want you to know I'm safe. The Agency ... they inject me full of anti-toxins so I can't get sick, no matter what. You understand?"

I nodded, my body humming with the need to taste him. "Anything else, or can I *hum lan* now?"

I don't know if he understood any Cantonese, but he seemed to get my meaning. His lips parted and he nodded. "Yeah, please."

Enough said. I scooted down and took his thick shaft in my mouth. Damn, if his lips were delicious, his *lok chat* was one of the best things I'd ever tasted. I sucked the head furiously but gently, my tongue smoothing over the smooth lobes. A drop of precum oozed at the tip, and I lapped it up, reveling in his salty sweet superhero flavor.

Encouraged by his groans and his fingers tightening in my hair, I lapped at his shaft, the skin like silk against my tongue. I suckled his balls and spread his ass open, feathering the tip of my tongue over his sweet puckered hole.

"Damnit," he growled, and suddenly, he pulled away. For a split second I became frightened I'd done something wrong, but in the next second I found myself flipped onto my back, Liam fitting his huge body between my legs.

I wrapped my legs around his slim hips and let him invade me. He wet his hand with his tongue and smoothed it over my bottom, pushing his large fingers slowly inside my ass, spreading me open. I threw my head back and groaned, unable to do anything else, overwhelmed as I was by this most incredible fantasy of a lifetime.

His cock was still really wet from my sucking him, and he pushed the head in my tight hole. A blinding flash of pleasure pain stabbed through me, and I groaned, my body weak and pliant underneath The Hummingbird.

"Is that OK?" I heard him whisper.

I grasped his arms and thrust my hips at him, trying to drive him in deeper. "Harder," I murmured.

His sinful lips curved into a grin, only making his flushed rugged face sexier than I could ever have imagined.

He growled deep in his throat and obliged, one slow but firm thrust embedding his cock deep in my tight passage.

My fingers tightened on his arms, bracing me against the thrust of his large body against mine. He moved slowly at first, gathering speed with each plunge, changing the angle of his cock so that he hit all the right spots. Sparks of pleasure danced up my cock, and the rubbing of his body against it was bringing me really close.

I slid my hands down to his hips, following the action of his movements, then to his ass. God, how I loved the way those muscles flexed against my palms, knowing it was from him being deep inside me.

He moved faster and harder, groaning, until I felt the hot gush of his cum inside me, his thick cock pulsing against my insides.

That did me in. One more rub against my cock, and I came, splashing against both our stomachs.

He collapsed on top of me, chest heaving. I put my arms around him, holding him tight against my chest, feeling our bodies stick together. His lips pressed against my neck, and even though he didn't say anything, I felt as if maybe he wanted to stay with me forever too...

*Stops writing and shifts uncomfortably in chair from raging hard-on incurred by memories. *

I think I'll have to work on the next chapter of our adventures later. That's when I'll go into detail of how Liam and I became inseparable and how he brought me to the Agency, got me the intense training that made me into a martial arts master (like my idol and look-alike) and sidekick to the love of my life. (Of course, my new career enabled me to pay off my debts and rebuild my father's store.)

"Kit."

Uh-oh. I turn at the sound of the sleepy voice and look in the direction of the bed.

Liam has turned over, his blue eyes sleepy, watching me, his rugged jaw covered with heavy dark stubble. My erection strains at the sight (as it does every morning). I set down my pen. Busted.

"What are you doing? Writing our daily log, I hope?" One dark eyebrow arches.

I think he's on to me. I nod. "Daily log. Of course."

"Good. Because if you're even thinking of writing that memoir you've spoken about, I'll have to give you a proper spanking."

A spanking. Hmm. My cock likes the sound of that, if the twitch it gave is any indication. Maybe I should fess up and take my punishment.

I rise up, woody jutting mercilessly, and cross over to the bed. Liam's musky scent fills the sheets, and I slide in, pressing up against him.

He turns over and I feel his cock nudge my thigh. His lips curve in a wicked grin. "You know I don't want you writing anything about me." The way he says that tells me he's definitely on to me.

Just before his lips close over mine, I return his smile. "Don't give it a second thought, Hummingbird. I wouldn't dream of it."

Kosher Man and the Shegatz

By Milton Stern

Mordecai was sunning himself on the roof of his building, enjoying the peace and quiet of a hot summer day. The temperature was to hit 100, but that didn't phase him as his people always vacationed where it was hot and enjoyed humid weather as well. Build a resort on the sun, and Mordecai and his tribe would be the first to make a reservation. After 40 years in the desert, they grew to love the heat. That may have been over 3,000 years ago, but Mordecai was as kosher as they came.

He knew he could enjoy the mid-day sun alone as he lay there on the chaise, wearing only a dark blue Speedo that barely concealed his more than ample package, and on his head, he wore his dark blue yarmulke with a white *Mogen David* (Star of David) embroidered on it. No one else in his building enjoyed the heat, and in all the years he lived there, he never saw anyone come up to the roof in the summer.

Mordecai was tall, over six-foot-four, with very broad shoulders, large, naturally hairless pecs, six-pack abs, bulging biceps, and powerfully muscular legs, all covered in dark olive skin, which at the moment was glistening with olive oil. Mordecai never needed sunscreen as he never burned. He was also known for his rather round and hugely muscular *tuchus* – buttocks to all you gentiles out there. His feet, at size 15, were not only quite large, but also magnificently beautiful.

But, it was Mordecai's face that drew people to him. He had black, curly hair that he wore short except for the top, and at over 40, his temples were graying, making him look all the more distinguished. Mordecai also had thick black eyebrows, hovering over bright green eyes framed in double rows of lashes that gave the impression he was wearing make-up, and his prominent Semitic nose led one's eyes to his full lips and gleaming white teeth. Mordecai's innocent smile could melt the coldest of hearts and made all the *yentas* and *bubbies* want to pinch his cheeks.

On days like this, Mordecai cherished these peaceful times alone. By day, he was a cataloguer at the Jewish History Museum in Greenburg, a popular metropolis on the east coast that drew the cosmopolitan as well as the seedy. But, cities have a tendency to do that, and Mordecai didn't mind. However, when the sun set, Mordecai emerged from the basement at the Jewish History Museum and headed home, and at the first sign of trouble, he donned a white mask and dark blue tights with a large white circled "K" emblazoned on his chest, along with white boots and a flowing white cape to become "Kosher Man." Mordecai wanted to forgo the cape as it always got in the way, but his mother insisted, and a good Jewish boy always obeyed his mother. He also wore a dark blue *yarmulke* on his head with a white circled "K" as well (it was actually the flip side of his everyday *yarmulke*). His best kept secret was how he never lost the *yarmulke* while fighting evil even though one never saw a *yarmulke* fly off an Orthodox Jew's head during a wind storm either.

But, the cape was his biggest nemesis. Often when flying, it would flap in his face, making it difficult to navigate, or he would go to punch a crook and end up tangled up in the cape instead. Whenever Mordecai experienced these mishaps, he thought of the joke:

"What do you call a Jewish ballerina?"

"A klutz."

He thought the same applied to a Jewish superhero as well.

Mordecai could have lived a normal, quiet life, but he displayed special abilities from a young age. While still a toddler, he showed great feats of strength, lifting furniture and other heavy objects around the house. As he entered puberty, his body transformed without ever having lifted a weight or participated in sports. His mother insisted he read as one could get an eye poked out playing sports. In high school, coaches wanted him to play football, but participation in various geeky academic clubs precluded his lettering in any sport. Mordecai was relieved because he was aware that he sometimes did not know his own strength, and he was afraid he would more than poke someone's eye out if things got out of hand.

One day, when he was in college, he was late for class, and as he started to run across campus, he suddenly found himself airborne and gaining altitude. Startled at first, he held onto his books while extending one arm in front of himself to guide his journey, and within days, he mastered his new-found talent. Mordecai then flew home to show his mother, and she did not act surprised, for she had expected this day to come.

"When I turned forty, I knew I did not have much time left to become a mother," she told her son, after he landed in their front yard and sat beside her on the porch. "I prayed, and an angel appeared before me and told me I would have a son and this son would be very special. He would be one of the chosen ones. He would have abilities not seen for thousands of years. He would have the strength of twelve men, the wisdom of twelve rabbis, and he would soar like an eagle, yet have the heart of a dove."

Mordecai listened intently as his mother continued.

"But, the angel made me promise that no forbidden food would ever touch his lips. He would learn the Torah and honor his parents," she said. "I was told he would have one weakness and that he also would never father children of his own."

"Why would I never father children?" Mordecai asked.

"I asked the same thing," his mother answered. "The angel told me that if I wanted a child, there were sacrifices I would have to make and mine was to never be a grandmother. I asked if you would be sterile, and the angel said it was more complicated than that. So, I never pursued it any further. He then made me promise again that no forbidden food would ever pass through your lips."

"And, I have kept kosher for you, Mother," Mordecai said as he kissed her on the cheek.

Only a few months later, his mother presented him with his first getup as Mordecai referred to his tights. And, for the last twenty-four years, he has been Kosher Man.

The sun was baking Mordecai, but he did not care as the heat energized him. He thought about moving to Boca or Palm Springs, but figured he'd wait until retirement when perhaps another crime fighter would emerge to take his place.

Mordecai was starting to doze when he heard the yell of a man in fear. He sat up on the chaise and tried to hone in the location of the scream.

"Five blocks northwest," he said out loud. Then, Mordecai jumped from the chaise and headed for the door to the roof, opened it and disappeared down the flight of stairs to his apartment on the fourth floor. Within seconds, the window to his apartment opened, and a flash of dark blue and white few out the window toward the northwest corner of Greenberg. Mordecai often wondered why no one ever noticed him flying out his window. But, city people were so oblivious to their own surroundings.

Once airborne, Kosher Man scanned the city, and his cape again flew in front of his face. "*Vaysmir* with this *feshtungina* cape," he cursed out loud. He swept the fabric from his face, then he located the man in trouble. In an alley next to the Lost Tribe Bar, a blonde man was surrounded by four men dressed in jeans and black T-shirts, which was unusual for broad daylight, even in Greenburg.

Kosher Man slowed down and slowly descended upon the scene in the alley landing almost quietly behind the four assailants, except for the metal trash can lid he knocked over with the cape. The four men turned around.

"Oh look it's the caped kike," one of them said as he pointed to Kosher Man, laughing.

"Whom are you calling a kike?" Kosher Man said as he lurched forward, grabbed the insulter by the collar and slammed him against the wall, instantly knocking him out cold.

Within seconds, like a streak of light, Kosher Man had rounded up the other three men and wrapped them up in a water hose before they realized what hit him.

"Do you have a cell phone," Kosher Man asked the blonde man.

"Ye … yes," he stammered. "Who are you?"

Over twenty years in Greenburg flying around fighting crime, and Kosher Man was surprised someone didn't know who he was. "I'm Kosher Man," he answered. It was then that Kosher Man got a good look at the man. He was in his early thirties if that old with a thick blonde buzz cut, blue eyes, pale skin, but strong features. He was wearing a tight red shirt that displayed a fine physique, and he stood about five-foot ten. Kosher Man rarely went for the WASPy type, but he thought a romp with this one would be worth a few minutes of his time.

"What are you some kind of superhero?" the man asked.

"You could say that. Now call the police before these hoodlums get loose. I have a city to patrol," Kosher Man said as he prepared for take off, dramatically sweeping the bane of his existence – the dreaded cape – behind him.

"Wait!" the man yelled.

Kosher Man turned back to the man and looked at his pleading *gentile* eyes. "What? Call the police now," the superhero asked then ordered.

"Don't you want to know my name?" the man asked.

The Hebrew hunk thought for a moment, then answered, "That's OK, kid, something tells me I'll run into you again." And with that, Kosher Man took flight.

He figured the *shegatz* (male *shicksa*) with the *goyshka cup* (gentile brain) would forget to call the police, so he swooped down on the first police car he saw, told the familiar officers what happened and where to find the criminals, and with that, he disappeared into the sky in search of more damsels – or dam-boys – in distress.

At around 4:00 am, Kosher Man zipped back into the open window of his apartment, closed the window, and with a flash, stripped off his costume, hiding it in the secret compartment in the back of his closet. He then brushed and flossed his teeth and showered in a manner of seconds and climbed into bed hoping for a good three hours of sleep.

However, Mordecai awoke two hours later with a raging boner. Spending his evenings fighting crime, with the exception of *Shabbat*, which he spent with his mother, and his days at the museum, stuck in the basement cataloguing, he rarely had a chance to go out and troll for sex.

Now, his balls were swollen, and his twelve inches (seven inches around in case you were wondering) of circumcised kosher meat with its large purple mushroom head was leaking precum like a faucet, begging for release. Mordecai ran his left hand down his muscular torso and using the abundance of precum, slicked up his dick and started stroking. It only took a few minutes before he was shooting straight for his open mouth, as he caught all he could, letting the rest drip down his chin, only to scoop it up and swallow it as well. Mordecai loved the taste of his own cum almost as much as that of the few Jewish guys he was able to pick up when he had a few moments of free time.

He enjoyed a few more minutes basking in the afterglow and marveling at how is over-forty-year-old dick remained hard for quite a while before finally going slightly soft. Mordecai then climbed out of bed and took a long hot shower – rather than his usual supersonic one – before heading to work.

He had been in the basement for only a couple of hours, tending to his duties, when Sylvia came down, calling for him.

"Mordecai," she bellowed over row after row of books and artifacts.

"Back here," he answered, as he was looking at a piece of parchment through a magnifying glass while sitting at his desk.

Sylvia found her way back to his desk and stared at Mordecai. He was wearing loose fitting dark blue pants and a white oxford shirt that hung on his physique, being a size too large. On his head was the familiar *yarmulke*, and he was wearing his gray, plastic framed bifocals. (Even superheroes need reading glasses after a certain age, so when Mordecai's time came, he chose bifocals. This way he could continue wearing his disguise all the time.) Mordecai looked up at Sylvia.

"You know, Mordecai, sometimes you remind me of Clark Kent," she said with a smile.

He chuckled inside, wondering if she realized how close to reality she was with that observation.

"Anyway, Moshe called in sick," she continued. "And, I need to go to a meeting. I need you upstairs to be the guest docent for a few hours until I get back. The fresh air will do you some good."

"Now?" Mordecai asked.

"Yes," she said motioning him to get up.

Mordecai stood up from the desk and ducked his head as he worked his way through the cramped basement.

"It is amazing you have any color at all being in this basement all the time ... what has it been? twenty years?" she asked as she followed him upstairs.

"Yep," Mordecai answered as he walked upstairs to the main lobby of the museum, "but I sun myself on my rooftop on the weekends."

With a flourish, Sylvia left, and Mordecai stood in the lobby looking awkward as usual. He strolled around and straightened a few of the pictures, when the door opened and a blonde man walked in. Mordecai turned around and immediately recognized him – the victim from yesterday.

The man walked to the reception area, and Mordecai strolled over to greet him.

"Hi, how much to tour the museum?" he asked.

"Five dollars," Mordecai answered. The man handed him the money, and with that, Mordecai gave him a ticket and a tour.

"And that is the end of the tour," Mordecai said as he led the man back into the lobby an hour later.

"Can I ask you something?" the man asked, turning to face and look up at Mordecai. "What is your name?"

"Mordecai," he answered. "And what is yours?"

"Robert ... Robert Madison," the man answered as he extended his hand. They shook. "Can I ask you another question?"

"Sure."

"Will you have dinner with me tonight?"

Mordecai thought for a moment. In all his life, he never went on a date with a gentile. He hadn't even had sex with one. But, he figured it had been a long time since he did anything. "Sure, but we will have to eat at my mother's restaurant as I keep kosher and cannot eat forbidden foods."

"OK, where's that?" Robert asked.

"On 24th and H Streets, Mother Rose's Restaurant. I'll see you there at 8:00."

And with that, Mordecai had a date.

Mordecai arrived at his mother's restaurant a few minutes early. Rose had opened the restaurant soon after her husband died and Mordecai had moved to Greenburg. She knew her special son would only be able to eat strictly kosher food, and this way she could watch out for his diet without appearing to dote on him by cooking for him at his place or having him over for dinner every night.

Her eyes lit up at the sight of her only son, and at eighty-four, she was still in phenomenal shape, running her restaurant as she did the day she opened it twenty years before.

"Mordecai, shall I sit with you?"

"Actually, Mother, I have a date ... I think," he answered.

Rose looked concerned as she seated him at a booth in the back, the only one that could accommodate his large frame.

"With whom?" she asked.

"His name is Robert Madison, and I met him at the museum this afternoon," Mordecai said as the waitress placed a bowl of kosher pickles and olives on the table.

"Mordecai, you have to be careful with the *goyim.* There are plenty of nice Jewish boys out there ..."

"No, there aren't, Mother," Mordecai said. "Sometimes, I get tired of being alone. My life sometimes feels cursed ..."

"Don't you ever say that," Rose said as she sat opposite him. "Your life is blessed. You remember that ... and you be careful. A *shegatz* cannot be trusted."

"Mother, you're such a bigot," Mordecai said with a smile.

"I am not. I just think one should date his own kind," she said as she got up.

"Then I will date no one as I am one of a kind," Mordecai said, as he spotted Robert entering the restaurant.

Robert saw Mordecai and worked his way to the back of the dining room.

"Now here is he is ..."

"The blonde? He looks like an Arian," Rose said with shock.

"Mother!"

Robert walked over to the booth as Mordecai stood, and introduced his mother. She nodded, handed him a menu and walked away.

Dinner went smoothly, considering everyone in the restaurant was staring at them, and Rose appeared to be studying rather than observing the two men.

Mordecai went to pay the bill, but his mother would have none of it, so he left the equivalent as the tip, and he and Robert left the restaurant.

"Where to now?" Robert asked.

"Well, I have an early day tomorrow ..."

"Don't be silly, come to my place for a drink ..."

"I don't drink," Mordecai quickly answered. "My people always eat, but rarely drink."

"Mordecai, that was my way of getting you to my apartment to have a little fun," Robert said with a smile.

"Oh," Mordecai said naively.

"You don't get out much, do you?"

Mordecai didn't answer as they headed to Robert's apartment.

Once inside, Robert did not waste any time. He pounced on Mordecai practically ripping off the museum cataloguer's clothes as he drove his tongue into his mouth, and Mordecai did not resist. Robert then stepped back to remove his shirt, and his eyes popped as he got the first full view of Mordecai in nothing but a pair of white briefs.

"Oh my God," Robert said as he slowly undressed himself. "Who knew that under all that baggy clothing stood an Adonis?" He removed that last stitch, and completely naked, walked over to Mordecai and ran his hands all over the superhero's body, totally unaware that he had seen that physique before, only covered in dark blue tights and wearing a white mask. As he ran his hands up the back of Mordecai's neck, he went to remove the yarmulke, but Mordecai stopped him.

"That stays on," Mordecai said as he grabbed Robert's wrist. Mordecai then ran his hands down Robert's furry torso and grabbed his six-inch dick, which was raging hard. Not too large, but Mordecai always marveled at smaller penises, wondering what it would be like to be normal.

Robert grabbed the waist of Mordecai's briefs and worked them down but had trouble stretching them past the tall Hebrew's hard-on.

"Here, let me help you," Mordecai said as he eased his foot-long *shlong* out of his briefs before sliding them down his huge thighs and kicking them away.

Robert reached for Mordecai's kosher meat with his mouth agape and his eyes wide open. "I can't get my hand around it. This is the biggest thing I've ever seen."

Mordecai eased him over to the bed, and as Robert sat on the edge of the bed facing the Hebrew sausage, he tried to get his mouth around the baseball-sized head, but it was no use.

"*I am cursed,*" Mordecai thought. But his dick was leaking so much precum that Robert worked the entire shaft and head with his tongue and lapped up every drop of the delicious nectar, moaning and leaking himself at the same time. With one hand, he stroked the length of it, and with the other he felt every inch of Mordecai's smooth, powerful body.

Mordecai eased him on his back and worked his legs over Robert's head as he faced the *shegatz's* crotch. Six inches was fine for Mordecai as he could get the entire length in his mouth and enjoy every drop. Robert continued doing what he could with all that cock he was given to play with – stroking and licking – and his tongue found the sweet spot between the ball sac and the asshole, marveling at how hard even that was. He reached around and ran his hands all over Mordecai's enormous muscular butt, all the while moaning in total ecstasy as his cock was deep into the hunky Hebrew's mouth. Mordecai worked Robert's cock making it leak almost as much as his own while he rolled the gentile's pink balls in his hand. He then worked his mouth down to those balls and sucked them individually and together before working his way back to the leaking head and slurping up all that tasty non-kosher precum. Mordecai wanted to make it last, but he was so turned on by what Robert was doing to him and what he was doing to Robert that he could not hold out much longer.

With one hand on Mordecai's cock, one finger working its way into Mordecai's hole, and his tongue working back to the superhero's plum-sized balls, Robert managed to bring Mordecai over the edge. With a scream that was surely heard in all the adjacent apartments, Mordecai shot a load that splashed his own chin as he continued sucking on the gentile's cock. Spurt after spurt of his kosher spunk erupted between them before Robert also lost control and shot clear into Mordecai's mouth. Mordecai hungrily lapped up the *treyf* (non-kosher) treat and swallowed all he could.

Robert was satiated, and said, "Damn, that was hot."

But, Mordecai didn't speak. Still hovering over Robert, he started to feel a burning sensation in his gut, then he rolled off the bed onto the floor. He held his stomach and felt a pain like he never felt before. He started to cry out, then he began to convulse to the horror of Robert who didn't know what to do.

"Oh no ... what do I do ... Oh shit," Robert whined as he went to put on his jeans and located his cell phone. He was fumbling with it, when he heard a knock at the door. With a flourish, he opened the door, and who was standing there, but Mordecai's mother.

Rose looked at Robert who was wearing only a pair of jeans that he had not had a chance to button up then saw Mordecai, naked and crying in pain and convulsing in the middle of the bedroom floor. By now, Mordecai had turned almost red as his blood was starting to boil, and he was sweating profusely. Eighty-four-year-old Rose shoved Robert out of the way and ran to her only son, the son she prayed for, the son who was a gift, the son who was dying right in front of her eyes.

"What did he eat?" she screamed at Robert as she knelt beside Mordecai.

Robert stood there frozen.

"What did he eat?" she screamed again. "Say something. He must have eaten something forbidden. What kind of *treyf* did you feed him? I have to know! My son is dying. What did you feed him?"

"I ... I ..." Robert stammered.

"Answer me!" she screamed as she opened her purse.

"He ... he swallowed my ...,"Robert began. "He swallowed my ..."

"*Oy vay*! Just say it. He swallowed your load. Now what did you eat today? Did you have ham? Shell fish? Bird of prey? Answer me, I need to know!" Rose screamed.

"I ... had a ham sandwich for lunch," Robert answered confused.

Rose then reached into her purse and pulled out a syringe and a vial with purple liquid in it. While Mordecai continued to convulse on the floor, she drew some of the liquid into the syringe.

"Get over here and help me hold him down. I need to plunge this into his heart," Rose bellowed.

Robert hesitated.

"Now!" she yelled as he looked right at her.

At that point, he figured she may be over eighty, but she could still probably kick his ass. Robert hurried over and helped her hold Mordecai, who although in pain and clearly dying, was still stronger than ever. He held the big man's shoulders while she aimed for his heart with the syringe of purple liquid. She may have been elderly, but her aim was perfect. The syringe went straight into his heart, and she pressed the plunger, releasing the liquid.

Within seconds, Mordecai quit convulsing. He quieted down, and his skin went from bright red to olive again. His body temperature also started to return to normal.

"Get me a blanket to cover him up," Rose said to Robert.

He pulled a blanket off the bed and handed it to Rose. She covered her son from the waist down and then pulled her cell phone out of her purse.

"I may have changed his diapers and potty trained him, and I have always known it was a large one, but I don't think he needs to wake up and find his mother staring at his naked body," Rose said as she started dialing the phone.

"What was in that syringe?" Robert asked.

"Manischewitz Concorde Grape," she answered matter-of-factly.

Rose called her friend Gert, and with Robert's help, they walked Mordecai to Rose's car – a brown Eldorado. Before she got behind the wheel, Rose said to Robert who was still in a state of shock, "I am truly sorry, but you cannot see my son again. It is a matter of life and death."

Robert did not argue, as he understood. Well, he didn't really understand, but he also didn't want to witness anything like that again. He also never wanted to sleep with another Jew for fear he would accidentally kill him.

Rose spent the night at Mordecai's to be sure he was all right. The next morning, she lectured him, ending with, "Superman has Kryptonite, and you have *treyf*. If you ever eat *treyf* again, I cannot guarantee I will be there to save your life. Perhaps you should carry a Manischewitz pen."

"Yes, Mother," Mordecai said, then he kissed her on the cheek. He then looked up and cocked one ear toward the window.

With a flash and a whoosh that almost blew off her wig, all Rose saw was a dark blue and white streak go out the window followed by a crash of glass as he had forgotten to open it.

"What do you call a Jewish superhero?" she said out loud, while shaking her head and smiling, "A klutz."

Mental Agility: How the World Got Its Champion
By Jeremiah Bodkin

It's late Monday afternoon, and I'm fighting a maniac in a tank.

That's OK. That's good. I like maniacs. Seriously.

Generally, I find that maniacs – depending on how crazed they actually are – are so absolute in their plans for world domination that they tend not to let little things like logic get in their way. Things that might give saner, more rational people pause for thought and make them consider before they stride forth wielding their Doomsday Device or Armageddon Axe or Big Stick of Badness or whatever.

Take you or me for example. Suppose you came to me and said, "I have a marvelous plan to take over the world, which will definitely not fail and should that do-gooder hero, Champion, try to stand in my way, why then, I will blow him to pieces using a tank."

I would be forced, however reluctantly, to point out that your plan was a feeble one, not even worthy of such second-stringer villains as The Candle Man or Madam Mayhem. For even someone like me, who doesn't have the most academically inclined mind, can tell you that firing shells from a tank at a man who can manipulate the very air around him simply by thinking about it – well, as plans go, it ain't gonna get you honor and glory in the Supervillain Halls of Fame.

But, I'm kind of biased there of course – I would say that, as I'm the man himself: Champion! I don't know how I do this shit, but I've always been able to.

There I go now, see, as this week's lunatic cackles with glee and launches shell after shell at me from his little tank, I yawn and lazily disassemble each one as it comes within a few inches of my face.

When I say I've always been able to do this – actually it's been ever since I was fifteen. I realized I could control things with my mind. No idea how, I just could – the same way some kids have a natural affinity for the piano, or for programming computers or playing football. However, as telekinesis wasn't on the national curriculum, I didn't learn to hone my skills in the classroom.

Distracted, I catch sight of myself in the mirrored windows of one of the skyscrapers that loom over my crazed opponent and me. One part of my conscious mind is dissolving the treads on his tank and tying the gun barrel in an aesthetically pleasing knot. The other is gently persuading the molecules of the large rifle he thoughtfully placed behind him to stretch themselves around his chest and pin his arms to his sides, rendering him helpless. And still another is surveying myself, floating in mid-air.

The late afternoon sun bathes me in its rays. It highlights the silvery blonde of my hair as it blows gently around my shoulders and bounces off the gleaming spandex of my costume. Now come on – I don't care what the fashionistas are saying these days. What hero worth their salt doesn't wear spandex? You think Ultima would get the magazine coverage he does without his world-famous purple unitard, or that Ulysses and the Battery Boy would set so many hearts aflutter if they ditched the whole briefs-and-tights combo? You want to wear a kimono, go be a Geisha; you want to be a superhero – pull that spandex on, boy!

Vanity is no more desirable in a superhero than it is in anyone else – less, if anything. Still, I've never claimed to be perfect, and looking at my reflection now, aged twenty seven, hovering above the crowds of New York City as I bask in the warm sunlight, I just can't help but think to myself: damn, you look hot!

However, it wasn't always like this. Oh, no.

I told you I didn't learn to use my skills in the classroom. Well, that's not strictly true. Let's skip back in time a way. Come on – you know you want to!

So, here I am, back in my old school in the UK. Oh, yeah – I wasn't always a resident of good old NYC – I grew up in one of the duller parts of suburban England. What's the matter with you, didn't you buy a copy of my official biography?! Aged – ooh, let me see – I think it's maybe two weeks after my fifteenth birthday. No – that's it, three weeks and a bit – February 23. I remember the date because that was when Donna Jay announced to Toby that she was pregnant in front of the whole class and burst into tears. Still, forget her, this is about me, me, me!

Sorry – vanity again. Not an attractive trait, huh?

Looking around this schoolroom full of bored teenagers, which one do you think is me? Which one do you think is Champion – defender of the earth, Golden Boy of America, the world's first openly gay superhero, whose chiseled features, lean, rock-hard body and long, flowing locks have gleamed forth from the pages of a million newspapers, magazines and TV screens?

Let me save you the trouble. I'm the scrawny geek with the bad skin sitting at the back and hoping no one will notice him.

I know – shocking, eh? So forgive me if I get a bit carried away sometimes by the way I look now – many formative years of being kicked around and told how disgusting you are tend to make you a little punch-drunk when a way down the road you get your Ugly Duckling moment.

Well, this was the day it first happened. This is when I reached out with my mind for the first time and realized what I was capable of.

See that boy sitting in the second row from the front? Yeah, like you hadn't noticed!

That is Sasha Gooding.

Sasha the Great. Sasha the Mighty. Sasha who just has that certain magical thing that some lucky bastard teenagers are gifted with that makes them stand out from their peers. His hair falls effortlessly into the coolest style possible. The school uniform, which, as you can see, has the effect of making me resemble a sack of shit tied up in the middle with string, hangs on Sasha's beautiful frame as if a designer had run up a special, unique version just for him. Even the regulation gym kit, which could take some of the most physiologically gifted boys and make them look like misshapen lumps, makes an exception for the lovely Sasha.

Predictably, I loved him with the fire that only a lonely fifteen-year-old can. Look at me – my head propped on one hand, the other holding a wooden ruler that I'm chewing the end of distractedly. Tsk.

Now this, this is the pivotal moment. God, it feels like yesterday.

As Sasha shifts in his chair, his body twists toward me and ... I remember so well, it felt as if I couldn't bear it any more – sitting there, wanting to touch this beautiful, beautiful boy, who was just a few feet away. Then, half in a daze, as I stared at his crotch something started to happen.

Without meaning to, I reached out with my mind and began to unbutton Sasha's trousers.

So bad! I know, I know! It was unconscious at first, but then once I realized what I was doing ... I just couldn't stop myself.

Oh, don't look like that – I was a hormonally charged adolescent boy for God's sake! Listen, let me tell you something: you know how in those comic books you read growing up, superheroes never abused their powers – the Man of Might would never have used his x-ray vision to spy on Daphne Day; Cloud King wouldn't have dreamt of throwing out a quick downpour to drench Fiona Fox if she was wearing a tight-fitting blouse, that sort of thing?

Bull shit.

I take my calling – and yes, it is a calling – very seriously. But I can't lie – I'm not above using my mental powers for a bit of frivolity. When I first got to New York, and I was dating, more than one guy would find his glass of wine inexplicably leapt into his lap, or wonder why he felt as if he was being touched even though we were several feet apart from each other. And don't think it's just me – you should hear Mr. Malleable the Shapeshifter tell a few stories of what he's been asked to transform himself into in the bedroom. And of course, he does it – we might be super, but we're still human!

Anyway, back to Sasha. Oh, boy. Slowly, oh, so slowly, I'm unfastening the waistband of his trousers. As the button parts company with its eye I can hardly breathe. I've stopped chewing my ruler, and it slides from my grip and falls on to the desk. It's quarter to three in the afternoon, I'm fifteen years old, I'm sitting in the most boring lesson of the week, and somehow – God knows how, but somehow, I am using my mind to pull down the trousers of the boy I have had a crush on for longer than I can remember.

Flushed with a mixture of excitement, fear and arousal I strengthen my mental grip. I can't even begin to describe this to you; I suppose maybe it's the way you would strain to hear a sound in the distance or flex a muscle in the gym? No, no, that's wrong, that doesn't begin to cover it. Whatever. But, as I extend my consciousness and pull, the soft dark material moves further down and apart, and I catch a glimpse of Sasha's underwear – light blue boxer shorts. I didn't think it was possible for my heart to beat like this. I can hear the teacher droning away in the background, but all I'm concentrating on, unable to believe what is happening and unable to stop it, is lowering the zip of Sasha's fly.

Suddenly – aargh! I pull too far, wanting to see more. Sasha jerks in his seat as he feels something tugging below his waist. Shit! He looks down and his mouth falls open as he finds his trousers gaping.

I snap my head down and stare at the blank page I'm supposed to be making notes on. I'm blushing furiously, and I feel as if everyone in the room is staring at me. I try, try so hard to keep my eyes on the page, but I can't help myself. Raising my head slightly, I find Sasha gazing back at me, and the look he's giving me isn't good. He knows. Somehow he knows it was I.

Glaring at me, he yanks his trousers together. No one else has noticed a thing.

My heart continues to pound as I force myself to write something – gibberish, anything. My head is on fire, unable to comprehend what just happened. As the lesson ends, I dash out of the classroom. I'm fast – but not fast enough. Sasha catches up with me, grabs my arm and pulls me aside. Until this moment, I would have given anything to be in his presence, but now it's the last place I want to be.

"How did you do that?" he snarls.

"Do what? I ... I don't ... what do you mean ..." I stammer feebly, trying to break free of his grip.

"That was you in there, you ..." he looks down, and now he's blushing. "I don't know how you did that, but just ... just stay away from me, OK? Have you got that, you freak?"

I nod, terrified, and as he lets me go I run, desperate to get away from him.

After that, everything changed.

Every day my power seemed to get stronger. I was scared, but as I learned how to control it, a new world of possibilities began to open up to me. I found that if I pushed hard enough with my mind, I could even use it to fly, after a fashion. Like when you're swimming and you push against the water with your hands – you use the resistance to drive yourself along, right? Well, that's sort of how it is with me and flight. With one part of my mind, I can push myself away from the ground; with another I propel myself, carving a path through the air.

Yeah, it was a bit scary, but let's face it – I was fifteen years old, and I'd just discovered I could fly – come on! Fantastic!

I felt bad about what I'd done with Sasha. I'd like to tell you it was the last time anything like that happened ... but I'd be lying! Let's just say there was many a boy on the swim team in our year who was astonished at the force with which the water determinedly tugged his trunks off!

Any fears I had concerning my newfound talents paled in comparison to the terror with which I now regarded Sasha. Not a day went by in which I didn't wonder whom he had told, who knew about me.

And the way he looked at me made me feel like dirt. To be gay in high school, then to start developing powers beyond belief, then to have both of these things exposed when you use your abilities to try and undress the school heartthrob – that's a lot for a fifteen-year-old to handle. Oh yeah, and let's not forget – I was awkward, geeky and unpopular *to begin with*!

But hey – don't worry. Things got better.

Zoom! Back to the present, and I soar through the city, exhilarating in the feeling of my body riding the winds. Behind me is our Monday Maniac in his little tank. Poor guy. Must be a bummer to start off the week trying to take over the world and not even to make it past dinner time.

Showing off slightly, I slingshot around a fountain, and enjoying the response from the crowd, I lower our vanquished villain to the ground, gently depositing his tank outside the NYPD. The cops can take it from here.

I'm just about to shoot up into the sky once again, when I recognize someone among the crowd calling my name. It's Luke Wilson, leading reporter for *The New York Times*. I smile back. I've always got time for Luke. In some ways – a lot of ways, I guess – I owe him everything.

"Champion! That's the third costumed criminal you've apprehended in the last fortnight – do you think New York is becoming a focal point for people like this?"

I laugh. "What, nutzos like this guy? Yeah, I blame Broadway. Musical theatre drives people to crime, didn't you know?" The crowd, chuckles, appreciatively. The whole wise-cracking, smug routine is a bit lame, but somehow they expect it of you.

Luke smiles, knowing that he, too, has to play his part in this ritual of cheese. I don't mind if it gives him something to placate his editor on a slow news day. "Is that how The Terror Twins got started?"

"Na – I think it was too much daytime TV that did it for them. Bad business." I return his smile with a knowing wink. "Anything else I can help you with?"

"Perhaps before you go, you could tell us just what you attribute your own rise to? To what strange twist of fate do we owe the presence of our Golden Protector?"

OK, I feel my leg being pulled – that's one piece of cheese too far. Deadpan, I reply without missing a beat: "Why, Luke, to the love of a good man, of course."

He grins. The love-in is at an end. "And," I call back as I rise into the air once again, my cape flying behind me, "Let's not forget the importance of a good tailor!"

As I push upwards into the sky, amidst the whistles and cheers, there is one man at the back of the crowd shouting, "Ya flying faggot!"

I wave to some teenagers who are whooping just behind Luke, giving no sign that I'm aware of this man, nor of the fat, brown dog turd, which has mysteriously scooped itself from the gutter and is now hurtling toward his face.

These things happen.

I'd been in New York for just under a year when Luke invited me to his housewarming. We'd met through a mutual friend who put me up for a while when I first arrived.

I wasn't really in the mood for a party, but at the time, I was earning a pittance working in a bar, and with less than twenty bucks to last me for the next week, I was very, very hungry, so a housewarming with free food looked more appealing than it might otherwise have been. And it must be said the apartment itself was worth more than a second glance – huge and roomy with a roof terrace to die for.

I was glad I'd thought twice about coming. Not only did the prospect of eating something that wasn't packet soup or porridge fill me with excitement, but also I needed to get out. I'd dated a few guys since getting to New York, but

Luke's circle were unlike anyone I'd met before. Nowadays, the thought of being stuck in a room full of drunken media-types, all tanned to the nines and trying to out-label each other, is enough to make me take my own life, but to the gauche twenty-one-year old trying unsubtly to wolf his way through the buffet they seemed impossibly glamorous. Sadly the fascination wasn't mutual.

I was already, it must be said, substantially changed from the pallid, skinny creature I'd been at fifteen and could even have been considered quite good-looking were it not for a certain unease with myself that I still hadn't managed to shake off. Nonetheless, to the young gods at Luke's party, I was beneath their notice. A few beers down, I was ready to go home, and my host was trying to persuade me otherwise with talk of what debaucheries were yet to come.

As Luke tried to pull me back, I laughed, shaking my head, and my bottle slipped from my grasp. Ordinarily, I would have caught it with my mind, but my reactions were a little numbed from the alcohol. Bending to retrieve it, I was struck by the oddest sensation. I heard someone call my name, and as I looked up, there he was in front of me. Sasha.

He looked bemused, but I think my own reaction must have been more one of shock.

"I didn't know you two had met. Ah, but of course – fellow Brits!" Luke was looking arch, sensing he'd stumbled onto something.

"We ... we were at school together." I managed to croak.

"Naturally ... I expect you only have the one over there, don't you? Well, you look as if you have some catching up to do ... I'll leave you to it." He departed with a mischievous look at Sasha.

We stared at each other. Eventually, Sasha smiled. "Hello." The last five years hadn't diminished his natural charms.

"Hi," I mumbled. "How come you're here?"

"I've got an internship at the *Times* ... Luke and I go drinking together sometimes. You?"

"I work in a bar." Oh, dear. It's funny how certain events or people can transport us straight back to the most awkward phase of adolescence. "I mean, I know Luke through a friend."

"Right ..." OK – time to get out before I make an even greater fool of myself. "I've got to go ... early start tomorrow."

"You work in a bar. How early can they need you to start?" A wry smile was playing around Sasha's lips. Embarrassment turned to anger. I'd already had my fill of being sneered at this evening.

"Early enough. Bye." I headed out toward the roof terrace. This wasn't such a great move as there was no exit that way, but Sasha was blocking the front door, and at this point, just getting away from him seemed my highest priority. He, however, was not so easily shaken off and followed me outside.

"Don't run away. I want to talk to you." He went to grab my arm, just as he'd done that day outside the classroom, but I dodged away. He called after me, "Please ... just for five minutes?"

I was so nervous. I hadn't seen him for so many years, and he still made my heart turn over in a way that made me want to run. But he asked again, and Sasha is very difficult to refuse. So I followed him over to the hideous fountain that played noisily in one corner of the terrace and sat down behind it, out of sight of the other guests, waiting for him to ask the inevitable. And sure enough, he did.

"How did you do it?"

"Do what?"

"I want to know. I haven't told anyone, and I won't. But I want to know how you did what you did to me that day in school."

I drew breath to make something up, whatever lie was most convenient, but before I could stop myself, the truth leapt out of my mouth. I hate it when that happens.

"That was the first time I'd ever been able to do it. I was probably as shocked as you were."

He looked sideways at me and nodded. "I doubt that. Go on."

"Go on, what? That's it, nothing more to tell. That was the first time I knew about it myself. Look …"

Not even bothering to check if anyone was watching, I looked at three plant pots by Sasha's feet and watched them hop into the air and fly in a circle around his head before I set them down again.

"See? That's it, alright. Happy now?" I was surprising myself with my petulance.

Sasha pulled his legs up onto the bench. "How many people know you can do that?"

I sighed. "Till now, I only ever told one person, a friend. And she never spoke to me again. You're the only other one who knows."

"Really? But why don't you use it? You could do anything with a talent like that. Think of the people you could help."

"Yeah, right. Whatever."

"I mean it … you should think about it. What's the point in hiding?"

I looked shyly across. There was something I had to say. "Look … I just wanted … I'm really sorry about what I did to you that day. It was wrong, and I'm sorry."

He smiled. "Don't worry about it. It was a long time ago. I did want to know how you did it though. Don't think anyone else would have believed me."

"S'pose not." I exhaled in relief. I'd spent so long feeling guilty about that day in the classroom – more than I realized. To get a chance to be free of it after so many years now was a massive relief. Not to mention the weirdness of sitting here with Sasha Gooding – Sasha the glorious.

"So how's it work then?" I watched him as he languidly extended one leg back out in front of him and folded the other beneath.

"It's difficult to explain. I just sort of feel things with my mind."

"And so that day you ... what? Reached out and ..." he laughed, embarrassed. "Felt me with your mind?"

"Yeah," I felt my cheeks color again, but he seemed more amused than anything. "Like I said, sorry. What can I say ... you were hot!"

He snorted with mock outrage, "What do you mean, 'were'?"

"Ah, well," I said, "evidently the years have taken their toll on you."

"Ha, ha." He flicked my arm. Then, there was silence. Somehow, that action, small and playful though it was, had crossed a boundary. Both of us were silent for a few moments.

Then, he spoke. "You can do it again if you want."

Time stopped. I felt cold.

"What?"

"Touch me again ... if you want. Like you did before."

I stared at him, sitting just a few inches away from me in the darkness. My mouth was dry. It's very difficult when you get something you've wanted badly for a long time; your body almost seems to want to shake you out of it and tell you it can't be happening. But it was.

"Are you sure?"

"Do it."

I didn't need to be invited a third time. I stayed there, staring into his eyes, but as I did so, my mind reached down and unbuckled his belt.

I felt, rather than heard him gasp imperceptibly as I started to unfasten his jeans. At the same time, he extended his arm toward me and our fingers interlocked. My heart was racing. I could hear the water in the fountain behind us; somewhere in my head, I was dimly aware of the party inside, but it could have been the sound of a falling tower block, and I would have been unable to tear myself from him.

Still gripping my hand, he looked down and saw his shirt unbuttoning itself. As he raised one arm, the sleeve pulled back and off him, and with the other, he pulled me forward and kissed me.

Pressed against his naked torso, every part of me felt as if it were connected to him. As our lips parted, and we came up for air, I let go his hand and pulled off the rest of his shirt, while he tore mine over my head.

As he drew me into him once again, I felt his cock, hard through his jeans, and for a moment, I couldn't help myself. For a split second, my mind pushed us both away from the ground – it was no more than an inch or so, but he felt it.

"Jesus!" He looked down, alarmed. Guiltily, I smiled.

"What ... what else can you do?"

I toed off my trainers and socks, while my mind removed his own, and stroked his face.

"This."

Now I pulled him to me and as our lips touched once more, I lifted the two of us up. As we left the ground, Sasha broke from me and started to panic, but I held him. "It's alright ... I've got us. Enjoy it!"

He looked at me in disbelief, then joy as I drew us up further, slowly, slowly.

I wish I could tell you, make you fully understand how great it feels.

Hanging defiantly in the air we kissed again and again and held each other so tightly it felt as if our bodies would burst. As I yanked Sasha's jeans and boxer shorts down his thighs without touching them, wickedly I remembered that day, so many years ago. And as they fluttered to earth, I wrapped my legs around him and spun him away from me, my hand finding his cock as I did so.

When we slowly descended back toward the roof terrace, it's difficult to say which of us was the first one to notice the crowd looking up, open-mouthed at us. All I know is that I suddenly had a sensation of creeping horror – the power I'd kept secret for so many years was now laid bare for all to see in no small way. As were we. Shit.

I held us there above them, not knowing what to do. Then, as we hovered, naked, Sasha turned and kissing my cheek, whispered, "Well, it's done now – you can't hide anymore."

"No," I agreed, "I suppose not."

My body arcs gracefully, and I shout with joy as I burst up above the buildings. I am flying, the wind caressing every part of me in my skintight suit, the sun warm on my face. Can it get better than this?

Well, actually – yeah, it can!

Because, at the end of this afternoon of fighting a ho-hum nutcase, as I fly home, swooping in and out of skyscrapers and spinning through the air, standing there on the balcony of the penthouse apartment we share, tapping his watch expectantly and waiting for me with an ironic smile on his oh-so-beautiful face is Sasha Gooding.

Sasha the Great. Sasha the Mighty. Sasha my boyfriend.

I know – fantastic, ain't it!

I increase my speed as I see him, buildings flying by in a blur, and as I draw near to our apartment I reach out with my mind and lift.

Enfolded in my mental grip, he soars up to meet me and as our lips and bodies lock together once again, and we fly up into the darkening sky, I think to myself with a simple joy that I will never, ever lose: I am home.

Black Bull

By Desertmac

Toby Briggs was still flush from his sudden celebrity, and even hours later, was still a bit breathless from the abduction and torture by Arch Demenic and his subsequent rescue by none other than the Black Bull himself. Most of the reporters and cameramen had gone, and Toby was left standing in front of the police station wondering how, with no money or ID, he'd get across town to his college dorm room to get some clothes and then return the borrowed orange jump suit that they had loaned him when Black Bull delivered him, naked but safe, on the steps of police headquarters. He grinned yet again at his embarrassment, and his mind reeled at the recall of the bizarre and amazing day he would remember every single moment for the rest of his life.

He caught the eye of the policeman who'd literally taken him from Black Bull's arms two hours ago and said, "Ummm, Officer Armand, ummm, since my clothes and wallet were burned up, umm, I don't have my RTD pass or student ID, so umm, how do I get back to my dorm?" The campus was a good fifteen miles across the metropolis.

Officer Armand grinned and said, "I told you to call me Dan, kid." He looked at his watch. "My shift's just ended. I'll give you a ride home; just give me five minutes." Toby stood and waited outside. Officer Armand let him in his personal car, and as they headed for the campus, the officer looked over at him and said, "You've had one hell of a night, huh." Toby nodded as a weary smile appeared on his face.

Officer Armand had taken his statement, so he knew how Toby had been randomly abducted by Arch Demenic right off the campus and used to lure Black Bull to his trap, so he could finally kill the ubiquitous but elusive and mysterious superhero. Toby had been stripped naked, tied to some contraption, and a slow series of increasingly tortuous contortions had been set in motion that, if left to completion, would have mangled his body and literally ripped him to pieces. He had no idea why he was chosen to be the lure, but he was the most grateful twenty-year-old in the world when it worked. Black Bull had shown up just as the contortions were getting unbearable. He had fought an amazing, violent battle with Arch Demenic that had pretty much destroyed the warehouse around them and set the rubble ablaze. Demenic had realized he could not win and had escaped when Black Bull had taken the critical moments to stop the machine Toby was pinioned on before it broke any bones or ripped his flesh.

That was the story, and the officer believed every word of it – but he knew there was more to the tale than what Toby had told him and the press. He let the Auto-Drive pilot them toward campus on the busy streets and studied Toby's profile as he said, "No one knows anything about Black Bull. He just shows up and does his thing but never talks to the press. Everyone wants to know what his deal is; he's so mysterious." A little smile played across Toby's lips, but he only nodded in agreement. Officer Armand went on, "Y'know, I've read virtually every word written about him, all the witness accounts, even interviewed several people he's rescued. He's a strange one," he muttered, then pointedly said, "I know you had sex with him."

Toby's head snapped toward him, and his jaw hung slack as his eyes bulged with shock and fear. "Wha...?" He wondered how the cop could possibly tell something like that.

Dan smirked and said, "Don't worry, I didn't mention that in the report, and I won't say anything to anyone." In answer to Toby's unasked question, he said, "Spectrum Body Scan. When I did the scan, it picked up traces of semen around your anus and told me it wasn't Arch Demenic's, since we have his DNA on file ... but it definitely wasn't your average male's sperm, either."

Toby's face was scarlet, and he trained his eyes on the floor of the slow moving car. He didn't know how to respond to this, so he said nothing. The cop was a big, well built man with wavy black hair and piercing green eyes, probably late twenties, and very handsome. Toby assumed he would be a typical homophobic cop, though he had been nice, patient and understanding when taking the statement from the shell shocked and frazzled student – but he was suddenly very intimidating.

He put his big hand on Toby's thigh and gently squeezed. "Hey, don't get upset or scared or anything, kid; I'm not grossed out or anything about it. In fact, I'm ..." He hesitated, then forged on, "I'm very interested in what you did with him, how it happened. I'm very ..." He paused again, then finished in a low and kind of husky tone, "Comfortable with gay sex."

Toby's eyes darted to the cop's again, and several expressions worked their way across his face as he thought through the implications of that statement. He looked down at the hand on his thigh in the red glow of the dash lights. His heart raced, and his scalp tingled.

"I want you to tell me everything, in detail. It'll be our little secret, and believe me, Toby, you'll be glad to be able to tell someone what happened. I mean, from the way you talked about Black Bull, I can tell it was a good experience for you." He raised his eyebrows in question, though he'd made a statement.

Toby nodded shyly and tried to get his breathing under control. He was so conditioned to always cooperate with police that it didn't even occur to him that not telling the truth was an option. He began haltingly, "Uhhh, well, uhhh, you know what happened up to when he released me from the machine; everything I said was true." Dan nodded agreement. "Ummmm, I just left out what happened between then and when he brought me to the police station, and that it was about two hours at ... at his place."

He didn't know how to proceed from there. He had never talked about sex, let alone gay sex, with anyone before. Add to that the fact that his first sexual experience was with a superhero who was a huge black man-bull hybrid with the ability to fly and do all kinds of amazing things. It was more than he had been able to wrap his mind around when it happened, and he was still digesting it.

"Go on, be descriptive. You said you're an English major, so give me the details. I'm into this for professional curiosity, but also ... It gets me hot." He grinned lasciviously to encourage Toby. "Tell me the way you'd tell a story, a pornographic story, if you were to write it down."

Toby smiled at the handsome cop and relaxed considerably. "Well ..." He looked at Dan and glanced down to see that his mocha colored uniform was bulging in the crotch.

Dan shifted forward in his seat to give a better view and grinned even bigger. His hand was still on Toby's thigh, and the skin of the slender thigh was burning through the orange prisoner jump suit that so didn't fit the young man's fresh innocent face – but fueled some hot little fantasies of jailers and inmates in Dan's wholesomely sordid mind.

"He umm, flew us out of the burning warehouse, and I was like, so scared but so relieved y'know, and well, I was naked, of course." His eyes went dreamy as he recalled the scene. He almost forgot he was telling this to a cop, to someone he didn't even know, even though the cop had been so nice to him. "He flew us up to a penthouse apartment ... I recognized the building, too, but swore I'd never tell anyone, and I won't, even to you. Anyway, as we flew, I kept feeling the smooth black skin of his chest and stomach, how, you know, it was so smooth and kinda soft, but the muscles underneath were so hard and tight and flexing as he twisted his body to direct us. And it was so strange, how he has this short thick hair on his back and sides, feels kinda like a short paintbrush, and I would feel the hair where it ended and the smooth skin began, and you know, he's so amazingly strong and ..."

Toby couldn't get the adjectives out fast enough, jumping from one thought to another. "His face, his head, with the cross between a bull and a human, with those, like, four inch horns and the same hair as his body around his head and neck, but then he has a pretty much human mouth, and eyes, but his nose is, well, big, so the way it all comes together is, well, spectacular." He shook his head in awe. Then Toby laughed and relaxed into the seat even more. He nodded and said, "OK, you want the porn version? I've read enough stories on the net to know how I would like to tell one." Dan nodded enthusiastically, and Toby took it from there.

"He flew us in through a big window and laid me out on his bed. He did a kind of exam, to see if I was hurt, and luckily, I wasn't. So then he carries me in and gives me a bath in this big tub with spa jets, and the bathroom is beautiful, and he washes me all over ..." He blushed, then carried on, "And I got hard when he washed me there, and I was so embarrassed, but he kept washing me there, and after a minute I noticed his hand was still there and was just kinda, I dunno, caressing me and rubbing all over, underneath even, to my, hole, even." He was way too embarrassed to look at Dan as he described such things, but at the same time, he was really getting into putting all of it into words.

"I looked up into his eyes finally and, maaan, I got chill bumps all over my body. His eyes are so dark and deep and ... he had the most, I guess, hungry, look in them, but it was also ... sad." He went ahead and looked Dan in the eyes and said, "It was loneliness. Deep loneliness, Dan. I didn't know what to do, what to think, but I felt so drawn to him, as if I was supposed to love him, y'know? I've never done anything sexual with anyone ... yeah, a twenty-year-old virgin, I know." He nodded his head as if he was expecting the usual ribbing he would get when he admitted this to anyone.

"I looked over the edge of the tub and saw that he was naked, too, and hard. And let me tell ya, he was hung like a bull!" He blushed again and chuckled at saying a cliché that was literal in this case. "I mean, it was huge! And his nuts … bull nuts for sure, all hairless, black and shiny, hanging really low and swaying with his movements. He kinda spread his legs, so I could see it better, so I kept looking. I was so nervous and so scared, Dan. I mean, I didn't know what to do, and I was so unsure of what was happening. I mean, I knew it was getting sexual, no doubt, but this was Black Bull! He's this amazing superhero whom everyone talks about, who does all these amazing things to protect us, and he had just saved me from certain death! I dunno, maybe he can read minds or something, but he seemed to know I was gay and … well, I guess he is, too."

Dan stroked Toby's thigh and said excitedly, "I've never heard or read anything sexual about him before! No one knows what he does when he's not helping people. No one sees him anywhere else. Most folks figure he morphs into Black Bull when he's doin' his thing and is just a regular guy the rest of the time."

Toby shrugged and said, "That may be; I dunno." He shook his head as he thought back. "But he stayed Black Bull the whole time with me. Anyway, he was squatting there next to the tub, and I was looking at his dick, and then I looked in his eyes again, and he said, 'Does this feel good?' He was talking about his stroking my dick and feeling down around my butt, and I could hardly get a word out, but I said, 'Yes.' And he said, 'Do you like what you see? Does it scare you?' And I was, like, scared of it, y'know? So I said, 'It's so big, but it's beautiful.' Or no, I think I said, 'Powerful.' And he smiled. When he smiled, I got like, lost in his eyes, like I was hypnotized or something. He said, 'You don't need to be afraid of it. If you want it, it will work.' And I knew what he meant, somehow. I knew he meant that my body could handle its size, somehow.

"Then he took my hand and put it on his dick, and it was amazing. All these chills went up and down my spine, and it seemed as if electrical charges were shooting out of his dick into my hand. I just stroked it in awe while he stroked mine for a minute, then he stood up slowly, and his dick was right there in front of my face. I looked up at him, like for permission, and he nodded. I was so worked up I could hardly breathe! His dick was just as black as he was, and it was shiny, like, the skin was shiny and silky soft. I pulled it to my lips and licked up the precum that was leaking out, and it was so salty and so good. I mean, his dick was so massive, right there, and I was so turned on, but scared of it, even after what he said, y'know? But I looked up into his eyes and sucked the head in and started swirling my tongue around on it. I mean, I'd never done anything before, but as I said, I've read a bunch, watched a few video clips and spent many an hour fantasizing what I'd like to do to a man." Dan's eyes flared for a moment there. He grinned and nodded for him to go on.

"Then he held my head and pumped it in and out for a minute, which was so awesome; I mean, I was so happy to just give him complete control, cuz he knew what he was doing, y'know?" A little moan escaped Dan's throat, and Toby continued, "Then he held my head tighter and pushed that big black bull cock into my throat, telling me to relax, that it would fit just fine ... and it did! I couldn't believe that huge thing could fit in there, but it did, all the way down, which must have been all the way to my stomach! I was on my knees in the tub, splashing water around and hanging onto his really muscular thighs, and he was pumping that pole down my throat ... but slowly and gently, not all fast and rough like I kinda thought a bull would do it, y'know? But I was freakin' out, lovin' every second of it. It was my first time, and it was so damn amazing! I was about to cum without touching myself." He grinned and indicated his raging erection.

"But before either of us came, he pulled it out, lifted me out of the tub and dried me off with a towel, really gently and lovingly, as if I was some delicate porcelain figurine or something. He picked me up and carried me to the bedroom in his strong arms, and I buried my face in his neck and just breathed in his powerful male scent ... there's some porn type terms for ya." He snickered and winked at Dan, whose grin was threatening to clip his ears. "It was an even mixture between human and bull, I'd guess ... though I've never actually smelled a bull." He laughed.

"But it turned me on so damn incredibly, I was just tingling all over, and I was thinking, 'My first time is going to be with the one and only Black Bull! He's like, magical, almost mythical, since so few ever see him. And he wants me!' I couldn't believe it! I kept thinking this was all a dream, the whole thing! So he takes me to the side of his huge bed and just looks at me, like he's memorizing me or something. But I got scared when I looked down at that monster jutting out from between his legs and pictured it going in my ass, and he says again, 'Don't be scared, Toby. Just relax and let yourself go with the feelings, while I make love to you. I won't hurt you. I would never hurt you.'" He smiled shyly, and Dan tingled at the boy's innocence and vulnerability.

"And it was like he put this spell on me again, cuz I just looked in his eyes and then suddenly realized I was on my back in his bed, and he was over me and kissing me and I wanted his lips, and they were like, so big and his tongue was huge like a bull's tongue, I guess, and he just took over my mouth and my mind, and I was writhing around under him and starting to beg him to fuck my virgin ass like I was some slut!" He looked over at Dan as he sucked in a deep breath, while the car pulled into the campus entrance. "I mean really, Dan, I never thought I would be like that my first time! I was begging him to fuck me *now* and clawing at his rough, furry back with the big bull hump between his shoulders, and I could feel his wiry tail whipping around between my knees, and I wanted him so fucking bad, I was going out of my mind! By that time, I was humping up at him and demanding he stick it in!"

Both of them were achingly hard and wet spots were forming on their crotches. Dan pushed the privacy button on his Sportica SS, and the windows clouded over. He directed the car to a space outside the dorms and made it settle in place as Toby continued his tale.

"He was drooling so much precum, he didn't need any lubricant, so he aimed it and started kissing me again while he pushed it in. I have to say, it hurt some, but nothing like it should have, being that big and my first time. It didn't really feel good at first, but as I got used to it, it started feeling wonderful. It was only about halfway in at that point, maybe seven inches of it, and he just worked that much in and out for a while. He was saying how I was so beautiful and pure, and he was so honored that I was wanting to give him my virginity, that he would treasure this moment forever." He shook his head and squeezed his throbbing cock through the jump suit as he added, "He was so tender and loving about it all at first."

Then he looked over at Dan and was shocked to see that he had pulled his cock out of his uniform and was stroking it slowly, squeezing and releasing as he worked up to the head, then sliding his hand slowly back down in the ample precum. Dan's cock was pretty damn impressive, too – certainly not fourteen thick inches, like Black Bull's, but impressive on any merely human male. Dan snapped out of his trance and looked embarrassed for a moment, but then he just shrugged and said, "Please, continue. Don't mind me, kid; this is too hot to not do something!" He laughed and Toby chuckled nervously. He tried not to stare, but his eyes involuntarily darted down and over at Dan's cock every few seconds, watching the big slick head slide proudly up through his sinking fist then disappear in folds of wrinkled skin as his hand closed back up around it.

Toby was surprised that after all he had been through, as sexually sated as he had been and as tired as he was, seeing this hunky older cop brazenly stroking his big cock right in front of him while he told his fantastic but true tale of sexual exploration was getting him hotter than hell all over again. His ass muscles twitched, and he knew he was still somewhat sore – besides his whole body, from being contorted – but he couldn't help thinking he would love for this cop to fuck him, too. It seemed the black beast had awakened the beast within him, and he wanted more.

He stammered as he started up again, "W-w-well, then, w-where was I? Oh yeah. He was about halfway in and fucking me steady, and I was loving every moment of it. I mean, it was so much more amazing than any fantasy I'd ever had. I couldn't believe how good it felt to have this big part of this god-like man's body inside my body, y'know? And then he said, 'Now relax and I'll give you the rest of me. Don't worry, your body will handle it just fine. Something in my precum makes your body adapt and take it all the way with ease. I promise you'll love it.' So he pushed, and it did hurt a bit, but I trusted him and let myself relax, and then it was like I was high on something or hypnotized again, cuz I just lay there and let it go in and was tripping on how awesome it felt as I stared into his eyes. Before I knew it, his balls were resting on my ass.

"I couldn't believe that whole thing was inside my body, and I just felt so full and like I couldn't move, being impaled on something that big, y'know?" Dan nodded enthusiastically as he sped up his stroking. Then he reached over and unzipped Toby's jump suit with his free hand, stuck his hand in and groped for his cock. Toby gasped loudly and, not knowing how he should react, just tried to keep the tale going.

"Then h-h-he started p-pumping in and out, and I was like, in heaven, and I was begging him to keep fucking me, and he was moaning and kissing me and biting my neck, and I was holding onto his hairy body, and I reached up and held his left horn, and he went crazy, telling me how good it felt for me to feel of his horns, and he was fucking me like a wild animal," Toby was talking faster and faster in one unbroken sentence, "and I got hold of both his horns and held on, and he lifted me as he stood up and walked off the bed onto the floor with me still impaled on him, and he was thrusting up into me and picking me up and dropping me onto his cock and roaring like a wild bull, and I was screaming how good it was and to keep fucking me while I held onto his horns and …"

His next words were choked off when Dan lunged for his cock and swallowed it whole in one flash of movement. Toby sucked in a deep breath and bucked his hips up, feeling awkward for a moment when he realized he was searching around on Dan's head for horns to hold onto. Then he reached around Dan's side and down to find his cock. It wasn't hard to locate, and Toby started jacking it as Dan furiously sucked on his cock.

After a moment, he pleaded, "Let me suck yours, too? Please?"

Dan came up for air and smiled. "OK." He pressed some more buttons, and the backs of the seats hummed as they lowered and the console sank into the floor. The two seats became a small bed. They both pushed their suits down to their ankles and got in a sixty-nine position. As Toby took Dan's cock in hand and aimed it at his mouth, Dan said, "It ain't no fourteen-inch bull cock, but ..."

Toby grinned, mouth poised over the long, wide shaft and said, "You've got nothing to worry about, Dan, yours is still really nice, and very big. You have more than enough for me. My own isn't anywhere near this big."

Dan grinned even wider and said, "Oh baby, yours is just right to me ... and your ass, my god it's beautiful! When I saw your ass at the station, I just about came in my uniform! You're just right all over; damn near perfect, I'd say." They looked deeply into each other's eyes and smiled, both sensing a connection that was running deeper than just the sexual moment. Then they simultaneously plunged onto each other's cocks.

Their feeding frenzy lasted only a minute or two. They exploded into mouths and throats with the kinds of moans and body jerks that only powerful climaxes can trigger. After they sat up and kissed each other like lovers, Dan returned the seats to their normal positions, and they caught their breath as they pulled their clothes back on.

After a bit, he broke the comfortable silence. "So, what happened after you both, you know ..."

Toby sighed and slumped back in his seat. He spoke with a note of sadness, "I was lying in his arms and telling him how amazing and wonderful and sexy he was. Then I said, 'I think I love you.' He sat up and looked me in the eye and had that sad look in his again." Toby shook his head and his eyes welled a bit. "He said, 'Don't fall in love with me, Toby Briggs. You are a handsome, intelligent and very sexy young man, who has his whole life ahead of him. I cannot share my existence with another.' Seriously, Dan, he used the word 'existence'! He said, 'My life is a solitary one. Once in a while, I find someone like you … I have needs, but … I can't fall in love. Anyone I loved would forever be a target of my enemies. Years ago, I was in love. Arch Demenic found him, tortured him mercilessly and then killed him. I'll never forgive myself. Brian was the most beautiful and loving soul in the world; he was my world.' Tears came to his eyes and mine, too, Dan. It broke my heart when he told me this. I mean, I could see such bottomless pain and sorrow in his eyes; I'll never forget it as long as I live. I'll remember every second of our time together, but that moment was … God, it was so emotional."

Dan leaned across the console and hugged him. He kissed his head and said, "It is sad, isn't it. What it must be like for him. I understand him, in a way. I mean, I can't know what it's like to be a half-human, half-bull superhero, or have my lover tortured and killed by vile creatures, but I know what it's like to feel like I can't have anyone to love and hold and make love to."

Toby looked up into his eyes and asked, "You do? Why would you feel like that?"

Dan shook his head and muttered, "I'm a cop, Toby, and a closeted gay one at that. Gay guys don't tend to trust or like cops, y'know – and for good reason. Most cops are homophobic assholes toward gay guys. As soon as I tell most guys I'm a cop, they're gone with the wind." He chuckled bitterly. "Either that, or they're 'uniform freaks' and I just can't relate to them."

Toby rubbed his hand around on Dan's muscular chest and said softly, "I'm not that way; I won't run. I really like you, Dan. But honestly," he blushed and lowered his eyes for a moment. "I have had fantasies about cops. But you, Dan, you're better than any fantasy I ever had. You're so big and strong and sexy, and so nice, too. I'm hoping that ..." He stretched up and kissed his Adam's apple. "That you'll want to see me again."

There was a short silence, and Dan sighed pleasantly as he twirled his fingers through Toby's hair. Finally, he said, "It's late Friday night, and I don't go back to work until tomorrow night. Do you have any commitments tomorrow?"

Toby smiled up at him and replied, "No, no commitments. What did you have in mind?"

"Well, you could come to my place, and we could see where this goes."

"That sounds interesting." He smiled wickedly, then said to Dan's chest, "He did say that he might find me again someday, and we could have a night together ... if I wasn't spoken for by then. He said he would be very surprised if someone hadn't already won my heart by then. He said ... it's hard for me to repeat things like this about myself, but he made me feel so good, y'know? He said that I was special and would make the special one who lights the stars in my eyes the happiest man in the world. That's how he said it! I laughed."

"Don't laugh, Toby. I'm a pretty good judge of character, and having met you under extraordinary circumstances, I see exactly what he's talking about. And, look at it from my side: I'm going about my shift, doing my thing, when suddenly, a superhero lands in front of me and deposits a naked angel in my arms! I mean, if that's not a sign of something meant to be, I don't know what is!" They both laughed, and Dan caressed his shoulder.

Toby said, "Yeah. He could have given me some clothes, but he said something about the symbolism of bringing me there naked. I didn't argue with him, even though it was pretty embarrassing."

Dan shuddered as he felt drawn to the boy in a way he'd never felt in his life. He lifted his chin with his finger and looked into his eyes. "We don't know what the future holds, but I think we would be crazy not to give this a chance. Please, come home with me."

"OK."

* * *

Across the metropolis, in his beautiful penthouse, the black as midnight bull-man lay alone, staring at the ceiling, remembering the evening with the sweet college student, how he tingled when the boy looked into his eyes, so trusting, so innocent and so very hungry. He'd seen maybe first love in those eyes, or maybe just first hungry lust, but beautiful to behold, either way.

These deadly mind games with Arch Demenic had to stop. While he was winning most battles, he was losing the war. The deep, sinister connection he and Demenic had between their equally transcendent minds was what had enabled Arch to distract him with a disaster while he moved in on the boy first. When Bull had seen the boy in his dreams and knew they were destined to love, Demenic had plucked the image right out of his mind and searched him out before he could find and meet Toby, whom he hadn't even had a name to search for yet, just an image of him in his mind's eye, an innate knowledge of his soul – just as he'd had of Brian. He had found Brian, and they'd had a rapturous year to love each other, enough that when Arch caught, tortured and killed Brian, Black Bull felt as if his own soul died. He'd finally recovered, after three years, when he dreamed of Toby Briggs and felt he could love again. But before he could even meet him, Demenic had proved once again that he would destroy anything of beauty in Black Bull's life.

He lay there seething with resentment and rage, wondering if he could, or should, even bother going on, keeping the fight up, when he knew that as long as Arch

Demenic lived, he could never share his life with anyone. It had been the hardest thing he'd ever had to do – besides burying Brian – severing the mental link that connected Toby's and his fates, doing a furiously fast mental search and ultimately passing the boy into the arms of another man – a regular man, but a good one – who could protect him and give him the love he so deserved.

He held his arms across his chest and squeezed only himself. The huge black bull shivered and quietly sobbed as tears leaked out of his all too human eyes.

About the Authors

Armand – Armand works full-time and spends much of his free time writing erotic stories, poetry and fiction. He is currently working hard to publish his first novel and lives by himself in Ohio.

Christopher Pierce – Christopher Pierce is the author of the novel *Rogue:Slave*. His short erotic fiction has been published in every edition of *Ultimate Gay Erotica*, so far. Visit him on-line at www.ChristopherPierceErotica.com.

DesertMac – DesertMac lives in the Southern California desert with his partner of twenty-five years. He writes gay fiction that is posted on net sites like Nifty and RCWP, and has a website at: www.geocities.com/desertmac2000/.

Henry R. Kujawa – Henry R. Kujawa has been a comic-book fan since 1963 and addicted to superheroes since 1966 thanks to the Adam West of the *Batman* TV show. His work includes *2230*, a one-shot *MAD Magazine*-like parody of *Battlestar Galactica* (1984; now posted at the Zodiac Comics website); *Stormboy #1: Steal Your Heart Away* (currently available in six countries plus the Internet) and two projects-in-progress with Nick Cuti, a new Moonie (*Moonchild The Starbabe*) comic, and *Grub*, a sci-fi movie. Henry has been a member of KLORDNY, a "Legion of Superheroes" Amateur Press Alliance, since 1991.

Jay Starre – From Vancouver, Canada, Jay Starre has written for numerous gay men's magazines including *Men, Honcho, Torso*, and *American Bear*. His hot and nasty stories have been included in over thirty-five gay anthologies including *Daddy's Boyz, Kink, View to a Thrill,* and *Wired Hard 3*. His short science fiction story "The Four Doors" was nominated for a 2003 Spectrum Award.

Jonathan Clarkson – Jonathan Clarkson is a writer and actor based in the UK. Writing credits include a stage play about a murderous cleaning lady, numerous sketches for comedy shows on radio, stage and television, several articles for the defunct arts magazine *Watershed Down* and a sitcom that is currently in development. He has never worn a cape and tights, but believes he could carry it off.

Kiernan Kelly – Kiernan Kelly remains chained to the keyboard of a temperamental Macintosh, churning out stories of gay erotica. Don't laugh – it's not as kinky or as much fun as you'd think. Well, maybe it's a little kinky. Links to Kiernan's other stories and novels can be found at www.Kiernan-Kelly.com.

Mark Wildyr – Approximately thirty-five of Wildyr's short stories and novellas exploring developing sexual awareness and intercultural relationships have been acquired by *Men's Magazine*, Alyson, Arsenal, *Cleis, Companion*, Haworth, and STARbooks Press.

Milton Stern – As Managing Editor for Content Development for STARbooks Press, Milton Stern has edited his fair share of erotica, but this is his first foray into writing gay erotica. Milton has written two historical biographies: *America's Bachelor President and the First Lady* (2004) and *Harriet Lane, America's First Lady* (2005); and one novel, *On Tuesdays, They Played Mah Jongg* (2006). Milton's kitchen is orange and green with an Aquaman theme; his nickname is Clark Kent (if you met him, you would see why); and his favorite TV show is *Smallville*.

Ryan Field – Ryan Field is a thirty-five-year-old career writer who lives and works in Bucks County, PA. His short stories have appeared in many anthologies and collections over the past decade, and he is currently working on an upcoming novel.

Sedonia Guillone – Multi-published, award-nominated author, Sedonia Guillone lives on the water in Florida with a Renaissance man who paints, writes poetry and tells her she's the sweetest nymph he's ever met. When she's not writing erotic romance, she loves watching spaghetti westerns, Jet Li and samurai flicks, cuddling, and eating chocolate. She offers more delicious m/m erotica at her website: www.sedoniaguillone.com.

Stephen Osborne – Stephen Osborne has had stories published in *Hustlers, Best Date Ever, Dorm Porn 2,* and *Tales of Travelrotica for Gay Men 2,* all published by Alyson Books. He lives in Indianapolis with two cats and Jadzia, the Wonder Dog. He watches *Smallville* for the well developed storylines and the excellent acting and not at all for the shots of Tom Welling shirtless. Honestly.

Troy Storm – Troy Storm has had over 200 erotic short stories published under various pseudonyms in *Penthouse, Playgirl, Voluptuous, Honcho, Inches, Drummer, First Hand* and other magazines. His stories also appear in the anthologies *Men for All Seasons, Full Body Contact, Buttmen 2* and *3, Just the Sex, Fratsex* and *Manhandled.* This is his first dealings with superheroes, and he thinks those dudes are awesome – side kicked, front kicked or butt kicked.

About the Editor

Eric Summers resides in West Palm Beach, FL, where he works as the Senior Editor for STARbooks Press. He has never flown or worn spandex. Spandex is a privilege not a right, he says as he walks around the gym admiring all the wannabe superheroes. Summers is a former competitive power-lifter, who brags that he has not gone a week without working out since 1978. His friends say he needs a life. This is his third anthology for STARbooks Press, and Summers looks forward to editing more anthologies about musclemen, bodybuilders, superheroes, prisoners, military men, and even cowboys.

ng in the park. He was wearing these really tight jeans, so tight you

earing any underwear. "Excuse me," I said, having a hard time look

linded by that bulge in his crotch, "but don't I know you?" "Maybe,

ind of to   bout a

with Ray   God, y

t loser?   in?" he

aid. "Lik   s strong

ce body   e on G

illy, he l   s I ever

ı up to t   any ide

istaking   e sam

ı, I coul   ery lor

ood raci   ne swe

ing with   e in st

we go c   behin

ill see ı   in pu

ed?" he   vent to

privacy.   grabb

-hard. I

ck, traci   t, so f

ed it, ha

with m   bing c

bbing, I   n cock

he sound of unzipping filled the small space. I don't know who's h

, but before I knew it, I had his rod in my hand, and mine was in his

nt to do?" he asked, his tone challenging. I knew exactly, and sank